You Can Follow Me At:

Facebook Author T M Jenkins
Instagram Author Tina J
Instagram Tina J Presents
Twitter Author Tina J

www.tjpresents.com

In Love With a Miami Billionaire 2

TINA J

Foreword

The ones who love us the most, are the ones who will most likely betray us.

Previously...

ZAKIYA

"I can't believe you quit. Why would you do that?" Drina asked as we sat outside the restaurant having lunch.

"I didn't want to sis but come on. I would've rather stayed as just the housekeeper. He's the one who offered me a higher position."

"True but you were making great money. How can we afford to pay rent?"

"Girl, I can get a job anywhere." She snickered.

"Not unless you wanna work under him again." We heard and turned around to see Conscience. Her stomach was huge, and she still looked beautiful.

"Excuse me." I said.

"Do you mind if I sit?" She asked and both of us shrugged. Some guard pulled the chair out for her.

"Can I have a strawberry lemonade and a Caesar salad with no croutons?" She asked the waitress who rushed to get it.

"The bitch wasn't that fast when we ordered." Conscience chuckled.

"When you're the owner, they'll do everything a lot faster."

"OWNER?" Me and Andrina shouted. Conscience smiled and accepted her salad and drink.

"I know you ladies don't know much about me and my family so let me fill you in on a little."

"You can inform Andrina because she's about to have your niece or nephew, bonding y'all for life." I stood and tossed my napkin on the table.

"I'm done with Consequence." I picked up my purse.

"Sit down Zakiya." She barked.

"What?"

"You heard me. Sit down." She stabbed her salad and put the fork in her mouth.

"You don't tell me what to do." I snapped.

"Listen Zakiya, you are a great fighter but in no means to disrespect, you won't get a win over here."

"Who the fuck you talking to?"

"Zakiya please. Why are you snapping on her when she's only here to talk? I swear, Consequence got you mad at the world." Drina said pissing me off. His sister didn't need to know our business.

"Really?"

"I'm serious Zakiya. We didn't hurt you and I get it; he messed up but damn. She's only talking." I sucked my teeth and sat down.

"You have five minutes and I'm out." Conscience chuckled.

"You'll stay here as long as I want you to. If you have a problem with that, blame it on my brother. You should've never gotten involved with Consequence."

"You don't have to tell me. It's a mistake I won't make again."

"Zakiya Summers, you have the same attitude as I, which is why I find your nastiness funny. I can see how people view me when I respond the way you are." I rolled my eyes.

"Anything else, Miss Waters?" The waitress asked as she took away the salad.

"Yes. I'll have a rib eye steak, well done with mashed potatoes and a skewer of grilled shrimp on the side."

"Right away." She hurried off.

"Look, my brother likes you; a lot actually." I rolled my eyes.

"I doubt it. If he did, he'd be able to control his dick." I drank some of the water still left on the table.

"I agree and both me and my mother dug in his ass yesterday."

"Why is that?"

"For starters... He gave you a key to his house." She took a sip of her drink.

"Shit, as long as he fucked Lisa, she's never received a kiss from him, let alone a key."

"A kiss?" Andrina questioned, which made me curious.

"I'm sure when they were young he may have, but my brother has a no kissing rule if you're not his woman. I know firsthand, that he's never kissed Lisa after he turned eighteen."

"Whatttttttt?" Me and Andrina couldn't believe it.

"Nope. He said, kissing brings on emotions and he knew, him and Lisa would never be a couple and its no need to confuse things with her or any other woman." I smiled on the inside because he and I loved kissing one another. Does that mean he loves me?

"He's never shown her off or taken her on dates. Lauren is the only woman he's done that with and now you."

"Should I feel honored?"

"Any man who shows his woman off isn't to make her feel good about herself. It's to show his appreciation of who he's with. To show her, outta all the women in the world, he picked her. And to show her, he's willing to give her anything to make sure she's happy." I didn't say anything.

"What Lisa did is fucked up on all levels and I'm surprised you didn't beat her ass."

"I would never show my weakness to her." I thought back to the night Consequence told me not to let her see me cry.

I saw the satisfaction on her face as she told me about their indiscretion. I held it in and cried my eyes out in the office. I already fell for him and it hurt to hear he gave himself to someone else. So what he was with her for years. It was supposed to be me and him against the world.

"Consequence was happy you didn't because she'd play off it but let me tell you something about Lisa." I made myself comfortable. I guess listening to her isn't so bad.

"Lisa used to be our neighbor growing up. Her and Consequence shared things and have for years. He's never gotten serious with any woman besides Lauren and even then, something was lacking because he still fell victim to Lisa."

"Oh, I must be lacking something because he ran back to her." I sassed.

"To be honest, I thought that too." She gave me a fake smile.

"Then, I pulled my brother to the side and asked him privately what is it that keeps him in bed with Lisa and you know what he said?"

"I don't think I wanna know."

"Shit, I do. What he say?" Drina was all excited.

"Really?"

"Hell yea really? This is like a damn soap opera." She said making us laugh.

"He said, she's the only one who hasn't let him down."

"I'm confused."

"Consequence has had plenty of women growing up and each one never measured up to the woman he was looking for. They couldn't handle him sexually, mentally or emotionally. Then, Lauren came along and broke him down, only to break his heart so what did he do? Went back to fucking Lisa on a regular." I rolled my eyes.

"Then, you come along and challenged him in Walmart right away which took us all by surprise. Somehow y'all continued running into one another and you had him stuck. You didn't back down and it made him want you more. My nephew was almost kidnapped and you stepping in, sealed the deal."

"Then why is he so mean? Why did he sleep with her? I thought we were doing fine." I felt my eyes becoming watery.

"It's no excuse as to why he did it. I can say, he must've realized it was wrong because he left her."

"Left her?"

"Yup. She ran out my house yelling about him leaving her in the middle of them having sex and why won't he be with her."

"He still shouldn't have done it." I rolled my eyes.

"I agree."

"Then the bitch comes to my job." Conscience waved me off and accepted her food.

"She's run off a few women by showing up at places they worked at and Consequence didn't care. The only difference now is, he doesn't wanna lose you. He doesn't want lil Con to lose you."

"I would never walk out on lil Con."

"You already did. Excuse me. I have to take this. Wrap my food up." She walked away to speak on the phone.

"What did you do Zakiya. I know you didn't leave his son hanging." I put my head down.

"I have to go ladies. It was nice chatting." She grabbed her things.

"Oh, and it's been a week since it happened and lil Con has called you almost every day. I know you're upset with my brother and I get it, but he's not ok with you going ghost on lil Con."

"I just needed a break from Consequence."

"He's not asking you to be his mother Zakiya, we all want you to be very clear on that." She said.

"I know and I never said you guys did."

"To lil Con, you saved him and because you're around a lot, he wants to keep you around."

"I'm going to call him."

"Listen, if you don't wanna be with my brother, that's fine. As you can see, lil Con misses you. If you can't honor that, then it's best you continue not answering and never come around again."

"Is the truck out front?" She asked her guard.

"I think you'd be a cool sister in law but know hurting my nephew or brothers, will have a bullet in between your eyes before you can ask why it happened."

"Did you just threaten me?" I snapped.

"I only make promises. Enjoy the rest of your day ladies." She hopped in a black SUV and disappeared.

"I don't know about you but I'm ready to go home." I said to Andrina.

"Courage is outside waiting for me." I nodded. We paid for our food and stepped outside the restaurant. Courage was directly in the front.

"I'll be by the house in a few to grab some things."

"Ok." I spoke to Courage and watched them pull off.

"Who the fuck?" I barked when someone put their hands over my eyes.

"ROCK!"

"The one and only baby."

Consequence

"Daddy can we go see Miss Zakiya?" My son asked.

"Yea but not right now. Nana wanted to see you." I handed him his phone and locked the door on our way out.

"I know but I miss Zakiya."

"How about this? I drop you off to nanas house and go pick Miss Zakiya up. I'm sure she's gonna be happy to see you."

"Fine. Can you at least have her face time me?" I hated what my son was going through. A lot of it is my fault because I hurt Zakiya, but she still came around when I was mean to her. Why isn't she speaking to my son? It's been long enough so I guess it's time to go see her. The least I can do, is apologize.

"Hey. Have you spoken to Courage or seen Rock?" My mom asked when we got there.

"No why?"

"Conscience called and said she's having pains and neither of them are answering."

"Courage probably with Drina. I'll go by and check." I let my son hand go and my mom grabbed my arm.

"Don't go over there cutting up."

"What you talking about?"

"If Zakiya is there, let her speak first. You hurt her bad Consequence." She folded her arms across her chest.

"I know."

"I hope you do because now it's affecting my grand baby." I blew my breath.

"I don't doubt she'll be by to see him. I just think she's taking some time to herself. However, if she is home, just ask her to contact me. I'll handle it from there."

"A'ight." I sat in my car thinking about what my mom said. I don't think Zakiya is intentionally tryna hurt lil Con. But women take much longer to move past things.

* * *

I parked outside Zakiya's house and instead of barging in like I normally would, I picked up my phone and called. It took her to the fourth ring to answer.

"I just spoke to lil Con."

"He's been tryna speak to you all week." She got quiet.

"I told you, you didn't have to be the mother figure in his life, but you did it anyway. Now my son is upset because you haven't answered his calls."

"I'm sorry. I was hurt by what you did and taking a break." I heard the pain in her voice.

"Ok but you could've picked him up from my parents."

"You're right and I apologize again. I just told your mom I'm going to pick him up tomorrow. I can't believe I messed up with him. I love your son." I appreciated the fact she admitted to messing up and that she spoke to him.

"Come outside." I heard noise in the background.

"Why are you outside my house?" I noticed the shades move in her living room window.

"Do I need to come in?"

"No." It took her a few minutes to open the door and when she did, I became angry. I hopped out my car and rushed to the door.

"Why you dressed like this?" I pulled at the shorts barely covering her ass and the tank top. Granted, she had a thick robe on but still. What if my brother in there?

"I'm home and you've seen me wear this before." She tightened the belt on the robe.

"Exactly and I took them right off and fucked you."

"Consequence please stop. You asked me to come out here and I did. What do you want?" She blocked me from going inside.

"I can't come in?"

"I have company."

"Why my girl got company?" She laughed.

"I believe your girl is Lisa and trust me, she's not here."

"I came by to apologize. I was dead ass wrong for allowing her to touch me. You were my woman and I disrespected you, and us." Her head was down but I could hear her sniffling.

“I’m sorry Zakiya. I didn’t mean to hurt you.” I lifted her head and it was at this very moment, I knew I wanted; no, I needed her in my life. I wiped the tears from her eyes.

“Why Consequence? Was I not good enough? You could’ve told me.” I hugged her tight.

“I just messed up Za. I let my dick think for me. It’ll never happen again.”

“You hurt me.”

“I know and I promise to make it up to you.” I hugged her again and let out a sigh when she hugged me back.

“Damn I missed you.” I said lifting her face up for a kiss. I was surprised she allowed it to happen. Maybe the break she took made her realized, she needed me to. I swear if she takes me back, I’ll never cheat again.

“Ummm. I have to tell you something.” She kept her arms around my waist.

“What?”

“I didn’t know he was here, and I wanted to tell you about him.”

“Who? You didn’t know who was here?” She moved away.

“Yo! I gotta go.” Rock opened the door and my mind went crazy.

“Why is my sisters’ man over here?”

“Your sister? Rock, you’re with his sister?” Before he could respond, I placed the tip of my gun on Zakiya’s forehead.

“What the fuck you doing Consequence?” Rock yelled. Zakiya put her hands up and backed herself into the house.

"Yo! Put that shit down." He yelled.
"I told you never to cheat on me."
"I didn't Consequence; I swear. Rock is..."
BOOM! I didn't even stay to watch her body drop.

CHAPTER 1

Conscience

SAME DAY...

"Oh gawd it hurts." I shouted and grabbed the door handle. My car was parked away from the apartment and you'd only see me if you're looking because the area is dark.

"WHAT THE FUCK DID YOU DO CONSCIENCE?" I heard Consequence barking behind me.

"They were cheating on us. I have to get to the hospital." I felt the gun being snatched from my hand.

"You had no fucking right to shoot her."

"Your gun was on her Consequence. I just did what you couldn't." He snatched my hair and tilted my head back.

"Don't ever in your fucking life question my actions." His tone and facial expression scared me to death. This is the Consequence the world is afraid of.

"Consequence, you're hurting me."

"And you hurt me by possibly killing the woman I'm in love

with." He gripped my hair so tight, I thought he was going to rip it outta my scalp.

"You better pray she survives, or Rock won't be the only person you have to worry about." He tossed my head, making me hit it on the door.

"I won't apologize for finding out he cheated on me and..." He gave me a look.

"You have no idea what the fuck you talking about." He shook his head in disgust. Did he know something, I didn't?

"My water just broke." I looked down and my pants were soaking wet.

"Looks like you need to get to the hospital." He backed away, hopped in his car and left. Did he really just leave me?

"HELP ME!" I screamed out as loud as I could and one of the officers noticed me.

"Are you ok ma'am?" The officer ran over and noticed my wet clothes.

"My water broke."

"Ok there's another EMT pulling up. Let me grab them for you." I nodded and took slow breaths.

"Ok ma'am. Let's get you on the stretcher." The man lowered it for me and as they lifted it, Rock was coming out of the apartment.

When his eyes met mine, I saw hurt and anger. I thought he would speak or get in the ambulance, but he didn't. He asked which hospital they were taking me to and said he'd be behind us.

I rested my head on the stretcher and squeezed the rails as another contraction kicked in. Lord let me have a safe delivery.

* * *

"He's so handsome." My mom said holding my son. Rock stood off in the corner pecking away on his phone. He still had specks of blood on his clothes from the shooting. No one paid attention because it wasn't noticeable.

"Why aren't your brothers here yet?" My father asked still not knowing what transpired before we arrived.

"Mr. and Mrs. Waters, can I speak to Conscience alone?"

"Sure honey. I want to go call my sons anyway." She laid my son in the crib and her and my father stepped out. Rock closed the door and stood at the foot of the bed.

"What the fuck is wrong with you?" He barked.

"You said, you didn't know her and..." He cut me off.

"And I also said, I knew a woman with that name, and I haven't seen her in years. I go to meet up with a client at the restaurant and she's there."

"I know. I followed you."

"What?" His anger was building.

The phone call I received at the restaurant was to tell me Rock had left his house and in route somewhere. I didn't know it was to the same restaurant until another call came in, which made me turn around. I watched him get in his Phantom and drive behind Zakiya.

I waited outside the apartment to see how long he'd be with

her and was surprised when Consequence pulled up. He called her out and after they kissed, she attempted to tell him something and Rock came to the door.

I noticed my brother's facial expression and him reaching for his gun and crept over. I heard my brother say he told her not to ever cheat and she backed herself into the house. I went behind him and after seeing her in a robe, I put a bullet in her chest.

"I told you not to cheat on me." He chuckled and tossed his head back.

"You dumb bitch. Zakiya is my fucking cousin. Our mothers are sisters and we have the same last name." He shook his head.

"Why didn't you say that when I asked if you knew her?" I was confused on why he didn't just say that from the beginning. I never even thought to put two and two together, and I knew Zakiya's last name.

"Because I hadn't seen her and wasn't about to claim anyone. All you asked me is, if I knew her and never gave me any other information."

"This never would've happened if..." He ran over to the side of the bed.

"If you trusted me. Had you done that; I would've told you when I got home who she was. But you tryna be fucking G. I. Jane, shot her over your own insecurities."

"Well..."

"Well nothing bitch." He's never disrespected me, by calling me out my name. I knew he was upset.

"Bitch?"

"That's exactly what the fuck you are. DO YOU HAVE ANY IDEA WHAT YOU'VE DONE? DO YOU?" He shouted in my face.

"Your brother is going to kill you if she dies." He gave me that *you fucked up* laugh.

"Fuck him. He should've..."

"It's everybody's fault but yours, right? I should've told you this, or he should've told you that. Had you waited, none of this would be happening."

"Rock."

"Don't Rock me." He started pacing.

"My cousin, you know the one you shot. She had a rough life growing up. So rough you wouldn't have been able to survive half of it, and that was up until her mom disappeared with her at the age of 11." I could tell he was hurting.

"I hadn't seen her in fifteen years because my aunt moved, and no one could find her. We thought they were dead and now I find her, only to have my sons' mother, try and take her life. GODDDD! WHY DON'T YOU JUST FUCKING LISTEN?" He punched the wall and left a hole in it.

"You were everything I needed and wanted in a woman Conscience; everything, but you fucked up." He walked to the crib and picked our son up.

"I love you man and I'll be by to see you." He kissed his forehead and laid him down.

"You'll be released in two days because he needs to be

circumcised. Stay at your parents' house for a few weeks or until your brother calms down."

"I have my own house." He gripped my chin with his hand.

"My son can't leave the house for a few weeks and I will not visit him at your home. I'll be by to see him at your parents and once he can leave the house, we'll share custody."

"My son..."

"Our son Conscience, will be at my place and yours." He whispered into my ear.

"You may have money but that shit means nothing to a nigga from the streets. Fuck with me if you want." He loosened his grip and I snatched my face away.

"See you later man." He kissed him again and stormed out.

My parents stepped in and my mom had tears running down her face and for the first time in my life, I saw disappointment on my father's face.

"Why Conscience?" My dad asked and I rolled over on my side. I wanted everyone to leave me alone.

"Don't you dare roll over when we're talking to you." My mom snatched the covers off and stood in front of me.

"I'm gonna ask you one question and I expect an answer." I sat up.

"Was it worth it?" I shook my head no and burst into tears.

"You better pray Zakiya makes it because the way Courage made it seem, is Consequence is going to kill you, if she doesn't."

"They weren't even together." I said trying to make what I did sound a little less invasive.

"That means take her life because Consequence and her were going through something?" My father asked.

"No. I didn't mean it like that."

"We all saw with our own two eyes, how Zakiya and Consequence were with one another. They may not have admitted it out loud, but all of us knew what it was." My father spoke.

"You said yourself, once you spoke to her at the hospital when her friend was in the accident, you could tell just by speaking to her, that she loved Consequence. So don't you dare sit there and minimize their relationship." My mom was pissed.

"I messed up. I thought he was cheating, and he never told me who she was." My mom took my face in her hands almost exactly the same way Rock did and made me look at her.

"If a man cheats, it's because he wanted to. You don't take it out on a woman who had no idea y'all were a couple." She squeezed harder.

"They've never been in the same place together and if they had, it could've been avoided but it still didn't give you a right to shoot Zakiya." She let go with force and my head fell back on the pillow.

"I heard Rock say you'll be staying at the house." My father said.

"I have my own place..."

"Conscience Rose Waters, you listen to me and you listen good." My father never raised his voice at me.

"The man needs his own time to process what you did, and we agree with him having you stay at the house. If you don't wanna be there, fine. But in no way, will you deny him his right to be around his son."

"I wasn't..." He cut me off.

"You can leave when he comes, or stay in your room, I don't care. This is his son and he has every right to be around him. Are we clear?" I swear he sounded like Consequence.

"Yes."

"Good. Get some rest because you're gonna need it with a newborn." I pulled the covers back up and cried myself to sleep. Maybe I did mess up.

CHAPTER 2
Consequence

"I told you not to cheat on me."

"I didn't Consequence. Rock is..."

"She's my cousin man." I looked over at him and before I could pull my gun back, a bullet ripped through Zakiya's chest. I didn't see her body drop or call 911. All I wanted to do is kill Conscience. How could she be so reckless? Why is she even there?

When the ambulance pulled in the hospital, I was already there telling them she's my wife and I'll pay any amount of money to make sure she doesn't die. They tried to get me to leave but I stayed there all night.

Rock kept texting to find out updates because my sister was on another floor giving birth. I knew he was upset but he'd be more upset had he missed his son entering the world.

Zakiya had to be placed in a medically induced coma because when Conscience shot her, the bullet shattered pieces of her bones in her chest; meaning bone fragments were lodged in some of her muscles too. They had to cut her more than expected in order to get it all out. The doctor said she would be in excruciating pain and her body needed to rest.

For the next month, I sat in the hospital room and refused any visitors. The only people allowed in was, Rage, Rock, his mom and younger brother. Not only did I not want anyone to see her like that, I didn't want my sister returning to apologize. What she did was fucked up and right now its best she stays away. I didn't allow Andrina in either because she was a mess.

I felt bad for my brother Rage tho because Andrina miscarried and wanted nothing to do with him. He went to her house and surprisingly she moved back home. Not sure what made her do it, but she knew Rage wouldn't go over there. He could if he wanted. However, my mother told him to let her be. Losing a child takes a lot outta woman.

"You need to eat something Consequence." Rock's mom said and sat a plate down next to me.

Every day she visits and brings me food. Courage would bring me clothes and Rock had his barber come up to give me a haircut in the waiting area.

"I'm not hungry." She sat next to me.

"When Zakiya was young, I think she had to be around nine or ten. She'd tell my sister all the time, she was going to be a princess." She smiled.

"A princess?"

"Yea. She couldn't stand her mother."

"At nine years old?" I questioned. At that age, most kids are still latched on to their parents.

"You have no idea the drama my sister put her through."

"She wasn't raped, was she?"

"No, thank goodness. But let me finish." I nodded and listened to her story.

"She said and I quote, *"one day I'm going to meet me a prince like Cinderella and he's going to take me away from you. I'm going to be rich and have people waiting on me."*

"Rich huh?" I asked.

"Sadly, she never met him or at least we never met him, but she met you."

"I fucked her whole dream up." I chuckled.

"I haven't seen my niece in all these years and when I do, it's like this." I put my head down.

"I'm not blaming you or your sister and let me tell you why." I lifted my head.

"Your sister loves my son and unfortunately, believed he cheated. In the heat of passion, turned the gun on a woman she knew nothing about."

"It's no excuse. Conscience knows better."

"She does but when your mind is gone, you're going to see what you want." She scooted closer and held my hand.

"Zakiya's going to wake up and when she does, she'll want to know why? Why you left her there? Why did the thought of her cheating even cross your mind and most of all, do you still love her?" I turned to her.

"You love Zakiya, right?" I never said it out loud to anyone and here she is making me.

"Yes."

"Then be ready for the questions and be ready for her to fight or tell you she doesn't want anything to do with the man, whose sister almost killed her." I nodded and she let my hand go.

"You're gonna have to push that pride, ego and aggression to the side and be there for her. Her recovery is going to be hard and she's going to push you away, but you have to fight to save what you two had. If not, prepare yourself to see her with someone else." She patted me on the shoulder and stepped out to talk on the phone. I rose up out the chair and stood over top of Zakiya.

Looking down on her face she seemed to be at peace. Why would I wanna disturb it by being around when she opened her eyes? She's not gonna wanna see or be around me. I may as well leave her alone and allow her to move on.

I leaned down, kissed her lips and walked out the room with no intentions of returning. I even told the nurse there were no more restrictions on visitors. Conscience isn't stupid enough to come up here. Not after Rage and Rock ripped her a new asshole from what my mom says.

I sent a message to my mom, asking her to call Andrina and let her know she could visit. Zakiya needed to see her best friend when her eyes open.

* * *

"How you doing son?" My mom asked and sat next to me out by the pool. Lil Con and I were home and he asked if one of the kids who lived down the street, could come over to swim.

"I'm ok. Waiting for Andrina to tell you she woke up." She didn't have my number, but she did contact my mom.

"She sent me a text saying they gave Zakiya the medication to bring her out the coma."

"That's good to know." I said.

"What are you going to do?"

"Nothing I can do ma. She's not gonna want to have anything to do with the man whose sister shot her."

"You don't know that Consequence." I sipped the beer and looked at her.

"The two of you may not have been a couple for a long time, but you've been around one another long enough to fall in love." I sucked my teeth.

"I know it's hard for you to admit it after what the other bitch did but son, she's nothing like her. We were all able to tell the day she came for dinner." I stayed quiet.

"Actually, your father and I made a bet on how long it will be before you messed up with Lisa."

"Really?"

"We sure did." She laughed.

"He said, my son is strong, and he really cares for Zakiya and won't mess up. Where I said, Consequence is spoiled. He's used to getting what he wants, and Lisa knows exactly how to get him."

"I hope you got your money's worth." I took another sip.

"I did." She laughed.

"I thought you were gonna be stronger and push Lisa away."

"She's loyal ma. The only woman..." She cut me off.

"The only woman who will allow you to walk all over her. The one who has no morals for herself and thinks being a side chick or mistress makes her a winner. Son, look at me." I turned and kept my eyes on the boys in the pool.

"No woman is going to be ok with you having another on the side. I suggest you figure out if you wanna be a player for the rest of your life, or if you want a strong woman by your side. Someone to challenge you and say when you're wrong. And a woman who will love you past all the hurt you've been through. You have to let it go or you'll always be alone." She kissed my forehead and had the boys get out the pool.

"Nana. We wanna stay in longer." Lil Con whined.

"Fine. I guess no football then."

"I'm coming." My mom took them down to the Pop warner field once in a while to play with other kids.

The area we live in doesn't have a lot of minorities and they're the only two black kids around. They needed to play with kids who look like them anyway. I glanced down at my phone and it was a text from Rock.

Rock: *She's awake.* I text back thanks and let a grin creep on my face. At least, she'll be on the road to recovery and hopefully back to her old self.

"She's awake ma." I told her as she handed the boys a towel.

"Good. Give it a few days and go see her."

"A'ight." I went in the house and pressed the button to close the pool. I never left it open; scared my son would catch me off guard and fall in. I'd never forgive myself if anything happened to him; especially at his own house where it could've been avoided.

"How long you keeping them out?" I asked her.

"A couple hours. Why?"

"I'm gonna lay down for a few." She smiled.

"You need the rest son." She had the kids go upstairs to get dressed and shortly after, they left. I went upstairs, shut my phone off and passed out. My family knew the house number and had a key if it were an emergency.

The second my head hit the pillow; I was out. I hadn't slept since Zakiya was shot and now that she's awake, I'm going to make up for it.

CHAPTER 3
Zakiya

"What are you doing here Rock?" I asked after getting out my car.

He followed me from the restaurant. I had no idea he was even in the area. I searched my surroundings with my eyes because it felt as if someone were watching me. Their presence was felt; yet, no one's out here.

"What you mean what am I doing here? I run this state." He walked with me inside.

"Run this state?" I questioned and listened to him mention how he's the Connect in Florida and has been for a while.

"Why haven't we ever crossed paths?" He asked.

"I don't know. When we moved down here, I was young and stayed in. As I got older and mommy was spending more time giving people our money for drugs, I had to find a job. Five years ago, I moved on my own over in Liberty City manor and since

I'm always working, I barely go out. Not only is it always a shooting, I'm scared to lose my life."

"I get it. Let me take this call." He stepped in the kitchen.

I told him to give me a minute because I wanted to take a quick shower. I hated being out and coming home without being cleaned. All the germs and diseases people carried outside made me a germophobic.

"Put some damn clothes on." Rock barked when I stepped in the living room.

"This my house. I don't have to cover up." I joked and grabbed my thick robe and wrapped it around me.

"Anyway, what's going on with you cuz? I haven't seen you in years and ma, been looking for her sister. Where she at?"

"I have no idea Rock. One minute I see her and the next I don't. I can't keep up with her. I mean, the one time I did have a little money, I put her in a good rehab because you know insurance sends drug addicts to shitty ones."

"True."

"She stayed for three days and left. Arnie called and said he couldn't take it anymore and left her." Arnie is my stepfather and I loved him to death.

"I don't blame him."

"So what's this I hear about you and Consequence?" My eyes got big.

"How did you hear about him?" He chuckled at the same time my phone rang.

"Did you have to talk him up?" I picked the phone up and Consequence asked me to come outside. I did and everything was

going well until he saw Rock. I didn't even get a chance to answer him as the bullet ripped through my chest and I flew backwards.

"What the fuck did you do Conscience?" I heard Rock saying as he told me to stay awake.

"Fuck!" I felt him pressing down on my chest and yelling for me not to die.

"911, there's been a shooting. My cousin was shot in the chest." I could feel something wet hitting myself face. I figured he was crying.

"OH MY GOD! WHAT HAPPENED?" I heard Andrina screaming. All this was going on and I had yet to hear Consequence voice. How could he not speak or check to see if I were ok.

"Yo! What the fuck going on?" There's Courage voice.

"Zakiya please don't die. Please get up." Andrina was laying on me crying and all I could do is control my breaths. I've seen plenty of cop shows where people are told to take slow breaths, so you don't overexert yourself. If I planned on surviving this, I couldn't die before the paramedics had time to save me.

"Excuse us. Someone said there's been a shooting."

"Zakiya the paramedics are here now. You're gonna be ok." Rock said and I felt my body being placed on something hard.

"Please don't let her die. She's the only family I have. Please." Andrina was screaming. I went to open my mouth and closed it because it felt like I was choking.

"She's flatlining." Is all I heard before everything went black.

BEEP! BEEP! BEEP! BEEP! I heard and my eyes shot open.

"AHHHHH!" I screamed out as I tried to sit up. Well, I thought I did because there was tube in my throat and monitors all over me.

"Oh my God, you're awake." Andrina hugged me and I winced out the best I could.

"Shit. I'm sorry sis. Let me get the nurse." She pressed the button and a voice came over the intercom. I noticed her typing on her phone. I wonder who she's texting and if she's telling people I'm ok.

"How can I help you?"

"My sister woke up. Can you send the doctor in to take this machine out her mouth?"

"I'll page him now and someone will be right in."

"Thank you." Andrina put the button down and pulled the chair closer to the bed.

"She's awake. How are you Miss Summers?" A man in the white coat said. I lifted my arm the best I could and asked him to remove the tube in my mouth.

"Let me run a few tests on you and I'll remove it." I nodded and stared at Drina who had tears falling down her face. I squeezed her hand to tell her I'm ok.

A few tests later and the removal of the mouth tube, I was finally able to sit up but not without pain. I'm only allowed to eat Jell-O for now and they're monitoring my pressure. The doctor said it's been fluctuating and has now placed me on medication to control it.

"I'm sorry this happened to you sis." Drina squeezed my hand and cried.

"I don't know what happened. One minute I'm talking to Consequence and about to introduce him to my cousin and the next, I'm dying in my own living room." I said in a whisper but managed to get out.

"She did it because she assumed you and Rock were a couple. She followed you from the restaurant and..." She shook her head as she wiped her tears.

"Who? Who did it?" I never saw the person who took the shot because I was focused on the gun Consequence had on me.

"Their sister Conscience." My heart began to race, and the machines were beeping like crazy.

"You're telling me, the man I'm in love with allowed his sister to try and kill me?"

"He had no idea she was there and to be honest sis, we were all shocked."

"Is everything ok?" The nurse ran in.

"Yes, I'm fine." I wanted to tell her I wasn't but kept it to myself. My throat was hurting, and I felt tired.

"You know today is the first day, I've been allowed to visit."

"Why?" She laughed.

"Consequence had this entire floor on lock. For the last month, no one has been allowed up here and from what I'm told, he hasn't left."

"Then why isn't he here?"

"His mom told me, the doctor mentioned taking you out the coma and he felt, I should be here."

"I've been here that long?" They say you feel like you've only slept a day when in a coma, and they're not lying. I would never assume I was here for a month.

"Yea. Get some sleep sis. I need you to have all your energy when we leave tomorrow."

"Leave?"

"I don't think it's a good idea to be here longer than necessary. Who's to say she won't return to finish the job?" I nodded.

"Courage?" I asked where he is. She let her head go back and tears began to fall.

"I lost the baby Zakiya."

"No."

"I was scared you were going to die and couldn't calm myself down. I had a miscarriage the day after and I blamed him and his family. I told him to stay away from me."

"I'm sorry."

"It wasn't meant to be is how I look at it. If it were, our baby would've survived." She shrugged and I slid over the best I could so she could lay with me.

"We'll get through this Zakiya. You got me and I got you." I closed my eyes and let my own tears fall.

I cried for my friend who lost her child. I cried for my life because I almost died, and I cried because who knows if I'll ever recover and live the way I once did?

CHAPTER 4
Andrina

"Let me talk to you for a minute." I heard stepping outside my parents' house.

Ok, so I swallowed my pride and went home. Not because I wanted to but because I couldn't afford to stay in the apartment. My father doesn't even know I'm there because he barely comes out the room. He wakes up, my mom helps him clean up, he stays in the room and that's it. I doubt he's been down in the kitchen at all.

Anyway, when I asked my mom, she was skeptical at first. Courage scared her but once I told her we were no longer together she agreed. He claims I didn't need her but after losing the baby, I did. His mom came around and I appreciated her even more because of it. I've grown to love her like my second mom, which is why I stay in contact with her.

"Why are you here?" I asked trying to walk to my mom's

car. I haven't searched for a new one yet. He'd usually take me wherever I needed to go, or I'd hop a ride with Zakiya.

He stood there looking so sexy, and all I wanted to do is jump in bed with him. Him and his brother were very handsome, and women definitely threw themselves at them. To my knowledge, Courage has never messed up.

"Tha fuck you mean why am I here?" He moved from in front of his truck and walked over to me.

"It's been over a month and I get it Drina, I do. However; you're not the only one who lost a child."

"I know Courage."

"Do you know Drina because I think you forgot who was there when it happened." He barked.

"I didn't..." He cut me off.

"I watched the blood leaving your body or should I say my kid? I'm the one who raced you to the hospital and the one who had to comfort you. Not your mother or no one else; me. Then, I get you home and you yelling at me as if it were my fault."

"Your sister..."

"Fucked up. I know Drina but damn. You took that shit out on me. I wanted my child with you. Shit, I put the baby in there on purpose." He was angry and had every right to be.

"I wanted the baby too Courage. I didn't know how to handle the situation and... I'm sorry."

"Sorry huh? So sorry you brought yo ass back to your parents?" He pointed to the house.

"I didn't have anywhere else to go."

"Yes you did. You had me Drina and I would've never turned my back on you." He started to walk to his truck.

"Why you leaving?"

"I wanted to see with my own eyes that you were doing ok. You wouldn't take my calls or answer my messages."

"I..."

"I know when you felt better you were. I don't wanna hear that shit." He opened the door to his truck.

"You came to a toxic place all because you were in your feelings on something I had nothing to do with. You're weak Andrina and if I knew that before, I would've never chose you to be with."

"What?"

"You heard me. You're just like your mother. When the going gets tough, you retreat back to what you know instead of figuring shit out. How's it working out for you? Huh? Father still whooping your mom ass with one arm?" He shook his head.

"Take care Drina. I wish you nothing but the best."

"Courage?" I ran after him but he pulled off quickly. Why didn't I call him? He's right. He lost a child too and I was being selfish by not understanding his feelings. I assumed since he didn't carry the child, it didn't affect him. I was wrong.

* * *

"You ok?" Zakiya asked when I opened the door to Rock's house. It's where she's been staying. Neither of us wanted to return to the house we shared, nor did we have money to stay there.

"Not really." She closed the door and walked extremely slow to the couch. If her cousin knew she answered the door he'd yell at both of us.

"What happened?"

"Courage was outside the house yesterday." I tried to stop by here to see her but after work, I was very tired.

"How did he know where you were?" I gave her the side eye.

"True. They do know everything." She laughed.

"He told me off without being disrespectful."

"I told you to call him." I waved her off.

"I bet he's mad because you dissed him, and he went through the miscarriage with you." I sucked my teeth.

"Drina, men may not carry the child, but they do become attached. You two were together all the time. He had to be affected just as much."

"What up Drina?" Rock spoke coming in.

"Hey." I stared at him and had to catch myself. He's fine as hell too.

"Bitch, you will not have my cousin caught up in no shit with those other crazy motherfuckers."

"What you talking about?" I smirked.

"I saw how you looked at him and trust me; he's not over Conscience."

"Who cares? I just wanna have sex." I shrugged.

"Call Courage."

"He probably wouldn't answer. Anyway, you telling me to contact him; have you contacted Consequence?"

"No and let me explain why." I sat there listening to her reason.

"I'm still recovering and if I know him, he's unsure of how I'm dealing with the fact his sister did this." She pointed to the long scar going down her chest. It wasn't in the middle, but it was long, and inches from her heart.

"He's going to wait for me to be at 100% before he apologizes for her."

"You think so?" She asked.

"Yup. Plus, Rock told me he asks about me everyday. He told Consequence to stop by and he refused his offer too. It's how I know he doesn't have any idea how to handle it."

"Have you spoken to Lil Con?" She smiled.

"Yes. Rock brought him by and he stayed over. He asked a lot of questions and I answered the best I could."

"Did he ask who did it?"

"Yea. I told him to ask his aunt because she may know who it was."

"Bitch, no you didn't." I busted out laughing.

"Yes, the fuck I did."

"I'm going to see my son. You need anything?" Rock asked.

"How about me and you, have a one-night stand and..."

"Bye Andrina. I'll make sure to let Courage know you offering yourself up to niggas."

"Whatever. Fuck him." He laughed.

"You say that now but let him here you fucking someone else. I guarantee he kills both of you."

"Bye Rock."

"Oh, it's bye now." We all laughed, and he closed the door.

"You think he messing with her?" Andrina asked about my cousin and Conscience.

"He and I had a long talk."

"About?" I went in the kitchen to grab a snack. She still on liquid foods but I'm not about to starve.

"If I would be mad if he takes her back."

"Would you?" She shrugged.

"To be honest, I'm not sure. Yea, she shot me and everyone addressed it but is it fair to ask him not to love her? She thought he was cheating and..."

"Bitch, I know you not saying you forgive her."

"Oh hell no. I know how much he loves her, and I don't want him to feel some kind of way if he goes back to her."

"You know she'll be around tho. How are you going to handle her coming here?"

"He won't bring her here. Not while I'm staying in his house."

"You sure about that?"

"Positive. I already told him she gotta see me." She started coughing.

"I'm trying to decide if I'm going to shoot her in the chest or just fight." I noticed her having shortness of breath.

"What's wrong?"

"I'm having a hard time breathing." I dropped the snacks and picked up the phone to call Rock and 911.

"Andrina, I know I'm sexy and all, but it won't work." He laughed in the phone.

"Rock, something is wrong with Zakiya. She's barely breathing."

"Did you call 911?"

"Yea."

"A'ight. I'll meet y'all at the hospital." He hung up and I laid her on her side just in case she started choking.

A few minutes later the paramedics showed up. I explained that she'd been shot, and she began experiencing shortness of breath. They put her on a stretcher quick and rolled her out.

I locked the house up, jumped in back of the truck and took the ride. I kept telling her she was going to be fine, but she kept crying and saying she didn't wanna die. By the time we got there, I was a mess.

"What happened to her?" I lifted my head up and Consequence looked like he was about to cry himself.

"We were talking, and she couldn't breathe." He helped me out and ran in with Rock and the paramedics.

"She's going to be fine." I turned to see Courage standing there. I ran over and hugged him. It took him a few seconds to hug me back, but he did.

"Stop crying." He wiped my tears and just as I stood on my tippy toes to kiss him, the passenger side door of his truck opened.

"Hello Andrina; is it?" I moved away and stared at Courage. He went to open his mouth and I put my hand up.

"We're not together; right. I can't get mad."

"Drina!" He called out.

"Have a good night." I left him standing there. It wasn't anything else to say.

CHAPTER 5
Courage

"Why the fuck you get out? You did it on purpose but guess what?" I went to sit in my truck.

"She still winning because I'm dropping yo ass off and coming back." Ciara slammed the door to my truck mad as hell.

I was at her house getting my dick sucked. Yup, I sure was. It's been over a month and Drina made it clear that it's over. Ain't no use in sitting around jerking myself off when I could get this bitch to do it.

Anyway, my brother called saying something happened to Zakiya and if I could meet him at the hospital. I bust down Ciara throat, hopped up and bounced. The bitch followed me and got in before I could pull off. Not tryna sit and argue, I drove straight here. I didn't know Andrina would be in the ambulance. Shit, I thought Consequence finally broke down and went to see Zakiya and he brought her.

We've been telling him to visit but he's stubborn as hell and refused. He thinks she'll curse him out or blame him for it. Rock told him he'll never know unless he tries but again, he's stubborn and won't go. Yet, he rushed there after hearing she couldn't breathe. I'm not sure he'll stay when he finds out she's gonna be alright. At least he showed up.

"I just gave you head Courage. The least you could do is respect me. Damn."

"Respect you?" I laughed.

"How can I respect a woman who doesn't do shit? One who sits her ass at home doing nothing all day and thinks giving head to a nigga is gonna make him stay?" I switched into the left lane. I needed to get her nagging ass home right away.

"I'm sick of you Courage. You were mine before she came around." She grabbed the wheel making the truck swerve.

"Bitch, you crazy?" I knocked her head against the window, and it bounced off.

"You tryna kill me."

"I'm killing us. If I can't have you, the bitch can't either." I wanted to beat her ass.

"You possibly have my child in your stomach and sitting here saying, you wanna kill us. What the fuck wrong with you?"

"Nothing. Just get me home." I turned the truck around and sped to the hospital.

"Where are we going?"

"Don't worry about it." I made a call to Consequence and spoke in code the best I could without her realizing it.

"Let's go." I parked in the handicapped section of the hospital and hopped out.

"Why we back here?" I gestured for the two dudes in scrubs to come over.

"What's going on?" They spoke and gripped Ciara's arm.

"What the hell? Get off me." She yelled.

"Remember when you tried to kill us about ten minutes ago and then said, if you can't have me no one will? It shows how unstable you are."

"Courage."

"Therefore; you'll need to stay under suicide watch until you deliver."

"My due date isn't..." I cut her off.

"That's how long you'll be here unless you go in labor early. Peace." I walked in the opposite direction listening to her scream and shout and went straight to the bathroom.

* * *

KNOCK! KNOCK!

"I'll be right out." I grabbed some paper towels and started washing my dick off. It's no telling how long I'll be here for my brother and I don't want Ciara's slob on me.

"It's me Courage." I heard Andrina's voice and opened the door.

"Washing off her cum." She had her arms folded.

"Her slob yea; cum not all."

"Really?"

"You asked."

"I didn't expect you to be blunt." She rolled her eyes.

"You know me Andrina and I'm not sugar coating anything to spare feelings. If you wanna know did I fuck her; no. I did let her suck me off because I was horny and didn't want jerk myself. Anything else?" I zipped my jeans up and washed my hands.

"I'm sorry." Her head went down.

"For what?" I pulled down the paper towels and dried my hands off.

"Not understanding that you too were dealing with the miscarriage. I walked away and never turned back. I should've been strong for both of us. I couldn't tho Courage. I felt the baby move plenty of times and... it just died. I didn't do it on purpose. I'm so sorry I lost the baby." She just broke down.

"Is she ok?" A nurse walking by asked.

"She's fine." I lifted her up and carried her out to the truck. I dialed my brother up.

"She ok?" Consequence asked right away.

"She finally broke." I told him looking at her on my lap. She wouldn't sit in the passenger seat. My mother said, she didn't think Drina had really dealt with the miscarriage. Yes, she was upset but not to where she'd break down like just now.

"It's a lot. Tell her we got Zakiya and I'll hit you up as soon as the doctor tells us something."

"A'ight." I disconnected the call and allowed her to stay in my lap the whole ride to my house. When we arrived, I carried her in and started a bath.

"I'm sorry Courage. I blamed you because she's your sister." She had her head back.

"I wasn't even there."

"I know. I'm fucked up."

"Tell me what's really wrong Drina." She looked at me and started crying harder.

"She's going to have your baby and I'm not." I shook my head and removed my clothes to get in with her.

"She was pregnant before you." I sat down and she rested her back against my chest.

"I know but then I was, and you catered to me. What if she wants the same? I was scared she'd have the baby and you'll forget about me."

"You were with me damn near everyday and basically lived here. Why would you think that?"

"She kept taunting me about how, when the baby comes, you'll be with her."

"Taunting you?" I questioned and massaged her shoulders.

"Then, someone told her about the miscarriage."

"What?"

"She said it's my fault and that's what I get. Maybe she's right. Is this the karma for what happened to my father?" I made her turn around.

"Listen to me." I lifted her head.

"She's a scorned ex Drina. It's her job to piss you off. You just have to be strong enough to beat her at her own game."

"I'm weak Courage. You said it."

"You are?" She rolled her eyes.

"I'm not saying it to be mean because no matter how weak you are, I'll be your strength. It's what I'm here for but I can't do that if you're gonna run away every time." She started crying and rested her head on my chest.

"Did you sleep with her?" I made her look at me.

"I let her suck me off and that's it."

"Why tho?"

"Why you asking niggas for a one night stand?" Her mouth fell open.

"You thought he wouldn't tell me?"

"He's a damn snitch." She laughed.

"No. He knew you were hurting and tryna lash out. I'm happy he ain't one of those niggas who kept it to himself and did it."

"I would've probably cried doing it." She shook her head.

"I'm serious. All I want is you." She slipped her tongue in.

"Drina." I tried to stop her but since my man was awake and she slid down, I couldn't.

"Oh gawd. You feel so good." Once she started moaning, I had to handle her. We had a long night.

CHAPTER 6
Consequence

"Drina?" Zakiya called out. I lifted myself off the ottoman at the foot of the bed and walked over to her.

Last night, when Rock called to say she was having a hard time breathing, I rushed over. I hadn't spoken to her since she's been out and her cousin kept me updated; however, I wanted to see her. I felt the need to be next to her and make sure she was ok.

Anyway, the doctor told us it could've been her chest healing and muscles tightening. It's scary and because she panicked, it made her feel as if she couldn't breathe. I knew then, Zakiya had to stay under me so I could take care of her.

I'm not a doctor but I have one who'll come everyday to check on her. I even had a private ambulance I used at my clubs for people who overdosed, bring Zakiya to my house. It's the only way I knew she'd be safe.

"She's not here."

"Consequence?" She questioned and looked around.

"It's me." She sat up.

"Why am I here?" She asked.

"I remember this woman came here and said, if she ever got mad at me, this bed was big enough for her to sleep on one side and me on the other." She tried to laugh.

"How are you Zakiya?" Outta nowhere she started crying. I sat next to her.

"How could you think I'd cheat on you? Why weren't you there when I woke up? Where were you?" She started swinging and caught me a few times in the face. When I noticed her breathing heavy, I grabbed her wrists.

"I stayed there everyday Zakiya and I'm sorry for thinking you'd do me the same."

"I needed you and... and... you weren't there." I let her hands go.

"I've always been there Zakiya, even if you didn't see me." I moved closer and rested my head on her forehead.

"I'm so fucking happy you're ok." Her hands went to the side of my face and her tongue slid right in. I became aroused right away and stopped.

"You don't want me?"

"Hell yea, but you need time to rest and your body has to heal." She nodded.

"Consequence."

"Yea."

"I don't blame you and I never will."

"That's good to know." It felt good to know she didn't. It was weighing heavy on my mind.

"You can't control what someone else does." She said making herself comfortable.

"Just like you can't control how I'm going to react to her when I'm better. Goodnight." I smirked.

"Oh, can you bring me something to drink and then get in bed? I'm tired and I want you next to me all night."

"Bossy huh?"

"Lil Con said, his dad told him it's the only way to be when you want stuff done." I shook my head.

"You on a roll tonight." I headed to the door.

"Babe." She called out and I'm not gonna lie, I was happy to hear she still considered me as such.

"Yea."

"I love you."

"I love you too Zakiya."

"You better. I didn't let you taste my goodies just to like me." She smiled and changed the channel on the television.

"Let me get you something to drink." I disappeared out the room and smiled like the Cheshire Cat going down the stairs. By the time I brought it to her, she was snoring lightly.

I took a quick shower, threw on some shorts and laid behind her like she asked. I wrapped my arm gently on her belly and snuggled my face in her neck. She didn't have the perfume I loved on, but she still smelled good.

* * *

"Consequence, it hurts." Zakiya whined and her eyes were watering as the therapist watched her lift the two-pound weights above her head. I had to adjust myself a few times staring at Zakiya in the leggings that gripped her ass showing how round it was. The tank top exposed the scar on her chest and still, she was beautiful to me. From the top of her head to the bottom of her feet.

It's been two weeks since she's been here and today is her fifth day of physical therapy. She gave Rock a hard time when she was with him, so he never made her do it. Not me. I want her back to normal and if we have to push her, then it is what it is. I'll take the heat if it's going to help her get better.

"I know. Ten more minutes of therapy and you'll be done." I told her and the therapist walked over.

"But it hurts." The therapist had her arms lifted.

"You wanna get better right?"

"Yea but..."

"But how can you, if you're stopping and complaining."

"Can I do it with you." Lil Con walked down the stairs, put his game down and picked up the two-pound weight.

"You can't give up with him watching."

She nodded and let the therapist work her arms out. I counted for my son to lift weights and kept my eyes on Zakiya. He stopped and started doing what the therapist had Zakiya doing.

"Don't hurt my mommy." It's like the world stood still. Zakiya and I were both at a loss for words. I wanted to correct him, but she shook her head no and said we could address it later. The therapist didn't know us, and it really isn't her business.

"I'm ok. Look we're finished now." Zakiya said and took a seat on the couch.

"Thank you, Lydia. I'll see you tomorrow." I walked her to the door and went back to find Zakiya speaking to my son.

"Con, you know I love you?"

"I love you too mommy."

"Con, you know I'm not your mommy, right? Maybe one day, I can be your stepmom but to already have a mom."

"Where is she?" Neither of us answered.

"That's why you're going to be my mommy now. Right dad? You said, I could have whatever I wanted." Zakiya and I stared at one another.

"Nana said, people go to court and get kids all the time. It's what Miss Zakiya can do. Can we do it dad?"

"Consequence?" Zakiya called my name and I couldn't answer. My son is almost six years old and knows way too much.

"Huh?"

"What's for dinner?" She asked and it snapped me outta the trance I was in.

"Whatever y'all want."

"I want pizza." Lil Con said and kissed Zakiya cheek before running upstairs.

"I need a shower." I helped her off the couch and carried her up. The doctor and therapist said for her not to engage in strenuous activities and the stairs could be one.

"It's ok Consequence. He hears a lot and it was just a matter of time before he questioned it."

"I guess." I turned the shower on for her and peeled the sweaty workout clothes off.

"I see someone is turned on." She joked and stepped in the shower.

"You have no idea." I walked out, went to check on my son, came back in the room and locked the door.

"All I need is a hand job Zakiya. I can wait for sex." I told her after stepping in behind her. I couldn't take lying next to her and not being able to touch.

"A hand job?" She turned and lifted her leg as far as she could. I held it in my hand and allowed her to rub my dick up and down her pussy folds.

"I wanted more but if a hand job is all you need, then..."

"You're not supposed to... Got damn..." She bent over slowly and gave me full access to her open wide pussy.

"I'm gonna be quick." I was being honest. I hadn't had any in a minute.

"Fuckkkkk!" She yelled. I was in heaven too because she felt so damn good.

"I'm about to cum." Both of her hands were on the wall.

"Me too. Shit." I pumped a little faster and not too hard. I pulled out and she turned around to finish me off by squatting.

"Zakiya, you're not supposed to... Fuck." She suctioned her cheeks and pulled everything outta me.

"You needed that babe and I wanted to be the one to give it

to you." I carefully lifted her up on my shoulders and explored the inside of her pussy with my tongue.

"Don't stop baby. Right there. Yes. Oh, gawd yes." She squirted in my mouth and asked me to put her down because her chest started to hurt.

"I love you Consequence Jamir Waters." I smiled staring down at her.

"I love you too Zakiya Alyse Summers."

"Can you make love to me?" I lifted her head when it sounded like her voice cracked.

"Why you crying?"

"Because my body is fucked up now and it's only a matter of time before you get turned off."

"Never." I lifted her out the shower and started the jacuzzi. I sat down first and let her slide down slowly.

"This won't turn me away from you." I ran my hand down the scar.

"You sure?"

"Positive and if you wanted me to pay for plastic surgery; I will. Whatever makes you happy, know I'm the man to make it happen." She shook her head.

"Its been a long time since I've loved a woman and now that I have you, I don't wanna let you go." I wiped her tears.

"You're the woman for me Zakiya. Don't second guess yourself over a scar." She nodded.

"Now don't just sit there. Fuck your man and then I'm gonna make love to you later when Lil Con goes to bed."

"I wanted you to do it now."

"Nah. When I get you later, I'm gonna stay in it all night." She smiled and brought us to another climax. I definitely wasn't letting her go.

"I'll sign papers for him to be my son if you want." I stopped and looked at her. She was putting on pajamas and I had just slid my basketball shorts on. She caught me by surprise with her statement.

"You said, I wasn't going anywhere; right." I moved closer to her.

"Right. Zakiya, I need you to be sure though because its for life. There's no getting mad and asking me to take you off."

"I won't." Her arms went around my neck.

"A'ight. Let's go tell your son." She smiled and placed her hand in mine. When we got downstairs Alma was opening the door for the pizza guy. We sat at the table and had a family discussion.

CHAPTER 7
Rock

"Are you sure it's not too soon?" My mom asked Zakiya about adopting Consequence son.

"I've been around him six months or so and I really do love that little boy. If he wants a mother; why not? I don't plan on going anywhere and if I ever did leave Consequence, I wouldn't take it out on him."

"Look at how much you've grown. I can't believe my sister kept you away all these years." As usual, my mom started crying like the baby she is.

"How you feeling cuz?" I asked referring to her moving in slow motion.

"I'm better Rock. It's just hard on the therapy days. He's pushing me to get better and I understand, but am I wrong for not wanting to do it?"

"Wrong as fuck!"

"JULIAN! Stop cursing with these boys here." My mom

shouted and we all looked over at Lil Con at my ten-year-old brother Jackson. The two of them were playing that Fortnite game and paying us no mind.

"Consequence doesn't want you feeling bad about yourself which is why he hired you the best physical therapist out there. Never mind, he had the most expensive doctors taking care of you and your protection even for him to take a shower down the hall from your room when you were in the hospital, was outta control." She smiled.

"Zakiya, he may not say it as much as you want him to, but that man is in love with you." She started blushing.

"He's told me those three words, but it feels good knowing outsiders see it. I love him too. I don't know how he'll feel when I approach his sister." I shook my head.

Ain't no way in hell, I'm telling Zakiya not to retaliate. Conscience almost killed her and had Consequence not asked me to let her handle it, I would've done it myself. Not sure what, but I have a vivid imagination and me putting hands on her wouldn't have hurt as much as me doing other stuff.

It's been two and a half months since the shooting took place and I have yet, to really fuck with Conscience. She has gone home, and I pick my son up from the door. I don't go in, nor do I allow her in my crib if she picks him up from here.

I had Zakiya staying here at first but then she stopped breathing and her man wouldn't allow her to be anywhere but with him.

I didn't care for my cousin and him to be together because

he's a dog. Again, he's rich as hell so women see him as a meal ticket and do any and everything to get his attention.

As far as I know, the only person who hasn't is Zakiya and it's probably why he fell for her. She has no idea who they are as far as being billionaires or how much power they really have. I asked why he hasn't told her yet, and his exact words were, *I wanted her to love me for me and not what I could give her.* Sure shit, she loves him for him because other women allow him to do whatever and Zakiya ain't having it. He learned that when she left him alone for cheating.

"Do you need to seek revenge Zakiya?" My mom questioned.

"It's not revenge aunty. It's more like, she fucked up and the only way to make it right is for her to feel some sorta pain." She shrugged.

"Sounds like revenge."

"Revenge is if I'm going out tryna find bad things to do to her and I'm not. Consequence has me busy and so does lil Con. To be honest, I have no idea how I'll react upon seeing her. I may just fight her and get it over with; who knows? It's not on the top of my list of things to do."

"Well, I wish you get it over with because I don't like not knowing what's going to happen." Zakiya and I looked at one another.

"Neither do I." My mom stood.

"Be careful honey and protect yourself with him in the bedroom." She smiled.

"No kids right now. I'm still learning my bonus son and I'm not ready."

"No one is ever ready. Let's go boys." She called them in the kitchen.

"Aunty, lil Con can't have..." She cut Zakiya off.

"I know. Strawberries and bananas." She waved her off.

"Where you going?" She asked.

"To get my son. How long you staying?" She looked at her phone.

"It's 3:45. Consequence said he'll be here around five and then we're going to dinner. Will you be back by then?"

"Yea."

"Ok. Hurry up. I can't wait to see him." She hasn't been able to see or hold him because it was still too soon for him to come outside.

She's been stuck under Consequence every day and he's not even speaking to his sister, so he hasn't seen my son either. It's a lot going, and I hope everyone gets past it soon or it's about to be some lonely holidays.

* * *

"Can we talk?" Conscience asked holding my son as she opened the door.

"About and why isn't he ready?" I closed it and followed in the living room.

"I want to say I'm sorry for everything. The accusations

about you cheating, shooting your cousin and bugging out on you in general." She laid my son in his swing.

"It's all good." I grabbed my sons' bag.

"Rock, I don't know why I behave the way I do when you're the best thing that's ever happened to me. Well, you and my son." She pointed to the couch and asked me to take a seat.

"I had no right to follow you. It's just Lisa said..."

"Lisa? Since when you listen to that bitch?" I didn't care for her at all. She's been messy since I've been with Conscience.

"One day you were at the house and she came by to go shopping." I didn't ask when because it was normal for them to shop.

"She spoke of using the bathroom and mentioned overhearing you ask someone to find Zakiya Summers and how you missed the hell outta her."

"What?" I remember the exact day.

"I told her she was bugging but then Zakiya's name came up again, and you didn't say anything about her being your cousin. I put two and two together; or thought I did and figured you were cheating."

"There was no need to dip our Conscience. I told you over and over, you were all I needed."

"I know." She started crying and rested her head on the couch.

"I asked you again about her and you brushed it off. My mind went crazy. I confided in Lisa and she said, if he didn't deny it, then it's true."

"I told you when we first got together, she was bad news.

Conscience, an unhappy woman will cause turmoil and misery around everyone just to feel happy."

"Why would she do that to me? I've always been her friend and kept it real with her." She wiped her eyes.

"Again. She is unhappy and will try to bring you and anyone else down with her. It's why she went to my cousins' job. Lisa told her everything except the fact Consequence doesn't love her and will never make her his woman. The man doesn't even take her anywhere so why she felt the need to approach my cousin is beyond me."

"I'm sorry Rock and I know it's over but I'm still in love with you." I put my head down and blew my breath.

It's been fine coming here not speaking and ignoring the feelings we had. Now she tells me why things played out the way they did and how her love is there. How do I even react or what am I supposed to say?

"You don't have to say anything. You're dealing with a lot and maybe one day Zakiya will accept my apology."

"Doubt it." I chuckled. I stared at her wiping her eyes and remained quiet. I was lost myself.

"Umm. Are you keeping him overnight or...?" She walked over to get him. I hopped out the seat, swung her around and let our eyes meet.

"If you ever in your fucking life put your hands on my cousin for any reason, I won't come back." She nodded.

"If you ever if your fucking life accuse me of cheating again, I won't come back." She started crying again.

"And if you want this nigga in your life." I pointed to myself.

"You have a lotta making up to do." She wrapped her arms around my neck and jumped in my arms. I almost fell over.

"I love you so much Rock." The kissing was passionate, then aggressive and that was it. My clothes came off, then hers and both of us were moaning out for one another. Ain't no shame. She fucks me real good.

"Keep riding. I'm about to cum." I said guiding her hips and kissing her neck.

"No more babies right now so you'll have to suck me off."

"Anything for you." I allowed her to finish riding before thrusting harder underneath and jumping off.

"Yea Conscience. Just like that. Oh fuck." I moaned as she drained me.

"I love you baby." She said climbing back in my lap.

"I love you too. What the fuck?"

"What's wrong?"

"Your friend was at the window watching." We never made it upstairs and fucked all over the living room. Thank goodness my son was still sleep, otherwise he would've had us stop a long time ago.

"What?" She stood and threw her clothes on.

"There's no one here babe." She stood at the window and went to the door.

"I'm not bugging Conscience. She had her hands over her eyes watching through the window."

"She wouldn't do that."

"Go check the cameras." I zipped my jeans up and walked in her office. She booted up the Apple desktop and clicked on the security footage. Conscience covered her mouth when it showed Lisa arriving almost ten minutes ago.

"Why would she do that?" I turned her to me.

"How did she get passed the guard is the question?" She put her head down.

"What?"

"I told them they didn't have to announce her arrival."

"Conscience." I ran my hand over my face.

"I know Rock. She's been here almost everyday helping me with the baby and..."

"And now she's seen my dick, some of the positions we fuck in and..."

"What?"

"She saw that freaky shit you do." She shrugged. Conscience and I did some nasty shit to one another and I hated someone else saw. I'm not ashamed but certain things you wanna keep private and the bitch violated.

"I don't care. You're my man and I'll lick your ass, your toes, and the back of your kneecaps if I want to."

"But it's only for me Conscience."

"I'm sorry. I didn't know she'd do that and from now on the curtains will always be closed when we're together."

"WAA! WAA!" My son started crying.

"I'll get him. He's probably hungry." I told her and walked out the office.

"It's late babe. You wanna order something?"

"Yea. I'll take a shower when I'm finished feeding him." I said and saw the big ass smile on her face.

So much for bringing my son to meet Zakiya. I sent her a text and she said they were already home. She'll meet him eventually.

CHAPTER 8
Conscience

"Why you here?" Courage asked opening his door. He stood in the doorway not allowing me access in.

"I brought your nephew to mommy and stopped by to talk." He looked me up and down.

"I have to visit you over there."

"What? Why?" I tried to move past and he stopped me.

"My girl here and I'm not tryna break up no fights."

"Your girl? Why would I fight?"

"Because you almost killed her friend. She lost my child stressing and..." I put my hand up.

"Ok. I get it."

"I hope you do because you messed up a lot and my dick hurt from fucking so much to make it up to her." I turned my face up.

"Between you and Consequence, I don't know who's

worse. Ughhh, y'all make me sick." My brothers were blunt, no doubt. However, they didn't have to be that way with me.

"When you going to see him? I wanna be there." He laughed.

"Whatever."

"Your whatever attitude is why you're in the situation you're in."

"Babe, did the food come?" Andrina called out.

"Gotta go. She promised to strip and suck my soul out after we eat. Peace." He closed the door and I shook my head. Next stop. Consequence.

* * *

I parked in front of Consequence building and sat there. I knew he was here because his secretary said, he had a three-hour meeting this morning. I wonder if it were the one about opening hotels in California. Him and Courage said, they wanted to have more celebrities stay in the hotels and visit clubs. Word of mouth can do a lot for businesses; especially when it came from other rich folk.

I blew my breath and took the walk to the front door. I had access so I swiped my card and the glass door opened. Security smiled and pressed the elevator for me.

As the lights passed each floor, my heart began to race. My parents told me it's been long enough and it's about time to get this conversation over with.

"Hi. Miss Waters. How are you?" His secretary Mary asked.

She's worked for him since my father handed him and Courage all the businesses.

"I'm good Mary. Is he in a good mood?" I asked.

"He is. The meeting went extremely well." She smiled.

"Ok. Let me go see him." I walked down the hall and saw him speaking to his lawyer. His office was huge and had glass walls so you could see right in. He had a smile on his face which made me feel a little better. I knocked and his entire demeanor changed.

"Brock. We'll discuss this later." He dismissed his lawyer.

"Looking good Conscience."

"Thanks. You're handsome too." He licked his lips and moved around.

He was a sexy, hood and cut to the chase type of lawyer. He played no games when it came to my brothers, and his clientele is high on the food chain. He wasn't a billionaire, but he had hella money.

"Why the fuck you here?" He barked as I closed the door. He may have glass walls but it's soundproof. Mary or no one else needed to hear our conversation.

"Consequence." I stood there scared to death as he leaned back in his chair clicking the top of his pen over and over.

"Why the fuck you here?"

"You haven't answered my calls or messages. I even emailed you and nothing." He gave me that *you fucked up* chuckle that Rock gives me when he's mad.

"What am I responding to? You playing victim for shooting my girl."

"Your girl?" I questioned. No one told me they were together.

"Yea my girl. Zakiya. You know the woman you tried to kill over your insecure ass?" He dropped the pen on his desk and stood to pour himself a drink.

"I fucked up with Lisa at your house that night. I did." He took a shot.

"Had I not, maybe Zakiya would've had time to tell me Rock was her cousin and my reckless ass sister wouldn't have shot her." He slammed the glass down.

"How did you know they were related?"

"As I pulled my gun out, he said it. Since you weren't supposed to be there, you jumped the gun."

"I wasn't thinking straight Consequence. I'm sorry."

"Sorry huh?" He stared out the window.

"Do you have any idea what you've done to her?"

"Mommy said she's getting better." He smiled still staring out the window.

"She's experienced a lotta complications and ended back in the hospital."

"I thought since she got out..." He cut me off.

"The fucking bullet shattered bones in her chest Conscience. Did you really think she wouldn't have complications?" He shook his head. I felt like shit even more listening to him describe the things Zakiya is going through.

"I hid my feelings for her but the moment you shot her, I couldn't any longer. Watching them work on her as they brought her in the ER broke a nigga. And then seeing her hooked up to all those tubes and machines, had me shedding tears." I looked up at him. At this very moment, I knew he was in love with Zakiya.

"I sat in the hospital for a month hoping and praying she wouldn't blame me. Hoping she'd still want me, the way I wanted her." He turned to me.

"You really fucked my girl up physically and mentally."

"I'm sorry."

"I'm not gonna tell you her business but I will say this." He sat in the chair.

"I fell in love with a woman who challenged everything I stood for. Her attitude, spunk and overall cheerfulness has been shattered by a bitch who thought her man cheated."

"Bitch?"

"Have you ever watched a woman go from carefree, to scared, to leave the house because of her scar? Scared to leave because she can't move as fast as before? Scared to wear certain clothes because she's scared the scar would show? And scared to leave thinking other women will take her man away from her because she may not be able to perform the way she used to?" I felt my eyes becoming watery.

"You broke her Conscience and for that, I'll never forgive you." I let the tears fall.

"Zakiya is going to come for you." He said and picked his phone up that started ringing.

"I'll be right there." He spoke and disconnected the call.

"Where was I? Oh yea, she's going to come for you. I don't know when or how but she's coming." He smirked.

"You're my sister so I know you're not worried but I'm here to tell you." He stood and picked up his phone and iPad.

"With me as her man, you should be. Now get the fuck out my office." My eyes met his and I saw nothing but hatred and anger.

"Don't bring your ass around me again. When I wanna see my nephew, his father can bring him by."

"Consequence please."

"Get the fuck out my face before I snap your neck." This isn't the first time he's threatened me but it's the first time, I believed he would do it.

Well this didn't go the way I planned. I left with my tail in between my legs.

CHAPTER 9

Courage

"Who was at the door babe?" Drina asked coming down the stairs in just a t-shirt. I swear, I didn't know who was more addicted to sex; her or me.

"Conscience." I locked it and made my way in the living room.

"I'm not trying to start anything but why is she here?"

"You can't start anything unless I let you. Come here." She walked around the couch and sat on my lap.

"She stopped by because she wants me to speak to Consequence for her."

"For what? Did she say that?"

"No but I know Conscience and I know my brother. He's not speaking to her in which I don't blame him and she's tryna figure out a way to make him. If I talk to him, she thinks it'll soften the blow."

"What do you think?" I reached behind her and picked the remote up.

"I don't think it will because truth be told, Consequence is in love with Zakiya." She wore a surprised expression.

"No shit." She couldn't believe it. Shit, I couldn't either when he told me.

"He told me before she was shot. Its fucking him up more because he never really got the chance to tell her and she almost died."

"Wow. Who knew his mean ass could fall in love? Hell, I'm shocked you did."

"Who said I was in love?"

"Oh, you're not? Ok, then I'm not either." She tried to get up and I held her down.

"You know I'm in love with yo sexy ass." She slithered off my lap and stood to remove her shirt.

"You in love with this?" She stood there smirking.

DING! DONG! The doorbell rang.

"You gonna answer the door or stare?" She asked laughing.

"This is a better sight."

"Boy, go answer the door." She threw the shirt back on.

"Ain't no boy over here." I pulled my dick out and watched her lick her lips.

DING! DONG!

"After we eat, I owe you." I put it back in my shorts and went to the door. The minute I opened it, I wanted to shut it.

"Tha hell you want?" I barked at Ciara who stood there with both hands on the door breathing fast.

"How you get past my gate?" I barked and looked past her to make sure the guard is there.

"You know Robert lets me in."

"Yea, well I need to change that. What the fuck you want?"

"My water broke."

"Ok why you here? The hospital is the other way." I closed the door and Drina had her arms folded.

"What?"

"Babe, go get dressed." She said.

DING! DONG! Drina went to answer it.

"Why the fuck you here? Go get Rage." How she snapping on my girl when this her house?

WHAP! I heard and spun around to see who hit who.

"Bitch." Ciara yelled.

"Don't bring your ass to my house talking about you're in labor and then get mad because I'm here."

"Fuck you."

WHAP! Drina smacked her again. I busted out laughing.

"If you weren't pregnant, I'd beat your ass. Since you are, I'll settle for the smack. Just know after you deliver, we need to meet up."

"Rage, can you take me to the hospital?" She ignored Drina. Ciara ain't no fighter; yet, she popped mad shit.

"You better get there the same way you got here. Matter of fact, who let your suicidal ass out the hospital anyway?" I slammed the door in her face.

"Get dressed." I told Drina who laid on the couch.

"For what?"

"I don't know if that's my baby and if it is, my future wife needs to be present." She sat up.

"Rage, she's not going to be ok with me being there."

"And I'm supposed to care, why?" She shook her head and laid there. I snatched her up off the couch and forced her to get ready.

* * *

"She's not coming in here Rage." Ciara tried to shout as the nurse checked her vitals.

When I slammed the door in her face, she left and brought her ass straight her. I knew she wasn't ready to deliver because if she were, she'd never have the time to stop by my house.

"I can go outside babe." Drina tried her best to remain civil, but Ciara is always pushing her buttons.

"Nope. Sit right there." I pointed to one of the chairs by the window.

"Sir. If the mom doesn't want her..."

"Bitch shut up." I cursed at the nurse.

"Bitch?" She placed her hands on her hips and Drina stood. I loved the way she had my back.

"That's what the fuck I said. Now unless somebody asked you a question, I suggest you mind your business."

"Rage, I don't want that ho in here." I bit down on my lip so hard I could've drawn blood.

"Bye." I told the nurse and waited for her to leave.

"Don't fucking play with me Ciara. Drina is my woman

and as the person who's going to be around the baby, it's no reason she can't be in here."

"My son or daughter…" She attempted to talk more shit. I took the tip of my gun and jammed in her mouth.

"I'll blow your got damn brains out right now and have them take the baby. Now I said, she's going to stay while you deliver. Understood?" She nodded with tears flowing down her face.

I put the gun in my waist and saw a frightened Drina. She's never seen me react this way and I'm sure it scared the hell outta her.

"I'd never hurt you Drina." She took a seat and sat quiet.

"Is everything ok in here?" A doctor strolled in looking at us.

"We good. How long before she delivers?"

"It all depends on Miss Bronson." He put on a pair of gloves and moved in front of the bed.

"Miss Bronson, I need to see how far you dilated." Ciara nodded.

"You're going to feel some pressure." He did the exam and said she was eight centimeters. He started preparing for delivery.

"I'm going to stand outside." Drina attempted to walk out but I grabbed her hand.

"I want you to stay."

"I love you Courage, but this is a moment for the two of you."

"Did you forget we don't know if this is my kid?" She chuckled.

"You still don't want to miss the delivery just in case." She pecked my lips.

"Don't leave."

"I'm not." She went to the waiting area and I called my mom up to sit with her. I'm sure this is bothering her, but I wanted her to know without a doubt, nothing will change once the baby arrives.

Two hours later, the baby was born. I didn't hold him or anything. I requested a DNA and left.

The results were in the next day and come to find out, the child is mine. Drina and I went shopping for a crib, stroller and all that. I'm happy she didn't let Ciara run her away. I am definitely getting her pregnant and putting a ring on it.

CHAPTER 10
Consequence

"Hey babe." Zakiya said standing at the stove. Whatever she was cooking smelled really good.

"You know I love you right?" We've been official now for four months, maybe five or six; who knows?

"I love you too. What's wrong?" I leaned against the counter.

"The time has come for you to sign off on the papers."

When she said yes to adopt my son, we went to the courthouse the following day. I had Brock tag along because I didn't wanna make any mistakes on the paperwork, messing up the chance to have this go through.

There were a lot of questions I couldn't answer about his mother which made it better for us. I even informed them Lauren hasn't been around for almost five years and my son had no idea who she is.

Over the last month, we've been back and forth to the

court. Brock sat in each time and made recommendations as far as making sure if Lauren did ever pop up, she couldn't protest it. By the time he finished putting everything together, the paperwork made it appear that Zakiya was his mom.

"Ok. Where are they?" She wiped her hands on a paper towel.

"Right here but before you sign, I need to ask you something." I reached in my pocket and she started hyperventilating. I'm talking shaking and her eyes started to water.

"What the hell wrong with you?" She couldn't even speak.

"The manager at the hotel is going out on maternity leave. I wanted to know if you could run it until she returned." I handed her a new badge with her name on it.

"Is that it?" She patted the sides of my pants and pushed on my chest to see if something was in my shirt.

"Yo! What you looking for?"

"Nothing." She smacked the badge out my hand.

"Never mind." She moved to the stove.

"Did you think I was gonna ask to marry you?" She sucked her teeth.

"Whatever." I busted out laughing.

"We haven't been together long enough for me to ask you."

"There's no time limit on love. If it weren't tradition, I probably would've asked you by now." She spoke in a sad voice. I forced her to look at me to see if she was serious.

"You dead ass."

"I love you Consequence and I'm the mother to your son. Why don't you wanna marry me?" She got very sentimental.

"I know your ass not pregnant because you swallow all my kids, or I pull out."

"Why do I talk to you?" I laughed.

"What's wrong Zakiya and be truthful."

"I want us to be a real family and we can't if we're not married. I feel like we had a baby outta wedlock and..." I couldn't stop laughing.

"Consequence. Stop laughing."

"I can't." I grabbed her by the waist.

"If it's meant for us to be married, it'll happen."

"When because my dream is to marry a rich prince, and I know you have some money so I'm willing to compromise with that."

"Oh shit." I backed up.

"What? I thought my husband would be a billionaire or trillionaire." She shrugged.

"You don't want me if I don't have that?" She placed the fork down she used to flip the chicken.

"I'd want you if you worked as a janitor in the hotel."

"What would you do with a billionaire?" I sat on the counter with her in between my legs.

"I don't know. Maybe be my own boss of a company. Wait! I'd let my billionaire man spoil me and in return for his kindness, give him as many kids as he wants. I mean, it's all I can do because I'm broke." She chuckled.

"One day you'll meet him."

"Doubt it."

"Why you say that?"

"Duh. I'm in love with you and no amount of money from another man will make me leave you. I'll settle for a janitor if he makes me happy." I stared down at her.

"I really lucked up with you."

"I'm the lucky one. I mean, besides your attitude and smart-ass mouth, you're really a great man who loves his son. I think that's what made me fall harder for you. Watching the way you are with him and how you go outta your way to see he's not missing anything. You're the perfect father and lil Con is lucky to have you." She stood on her tippy toes to kiss me. I sat there with nothing to say.

I stared at Zakiya moved around the kitchen with ease. It's like she's supposed to be the woman of the house.

She's been working herself out in the gym downstairs and pushing herself with the therapist. We were both shocked when she asked for a bigger weight. Even though her body is still healing, every day I see her getting stronger. Zakiya is the strength my son and I needed in our life and I'd be a fool to let her go.

"Where's lil Con?"

"Upstairs. Jackson came over. I hope you don't mind."

"Not at all." I hopped off the counter and went to shower. I heard her call the boys to eat and told her to put my plate aside. I laid on the bed afterwards and lit a black and mild. I smoked once in a while.

"Whew! Those boys are a mess." Zakiya came in the room laughing, stripped and hopped in the shower.

"Alma took them out for ice cream." She shouted from the

bathroom. I walked in and picked her clothes up and placed them in the hamper.

"I was thinking Consequence." She had no idea I was standing there because the steam covered the glass walls.

"Thinking what?" I stepped in scaring her. I rubbed my hands down the side of her body.

"When the judge signs off on the paperwork, let's take lil Con to Disneyworld." I kissed the back of her neck.

"He's been there before."

"Not with his mom, he hasn't." I turned her around.

"Why couldn't I meet you first?"

"Probably because you were mean as hell and screwing everyone. Oh, that reminds me. Lisa sent me a message on Facebook reminding me that you slept with her as a married man and you'll continue while we're together."

"I'll handle it."

"I'm not sure I want you too. What if... Consequence." She moaned out when two of my fingers slid inside. I wasn't tryna have sex until the kids went to sleep but everytime I saw her body; my man rose to the occasion. And since they're out with Alma, why not now?

"I'll never cheat on you again. Do you trust me?" I curved my finger and let my thumb circle her clit faster.

"Yes... Baby I do." Her head went back as I removed my fingers and lifted her up.

"Tell me what you want Zakiya." I had her back against the shower wall with her legs spread out in the crook of my arms.

"I want you Consequence. Only you."

"You sure?" I rammed in making her scream out and dig deep in my arms.

"Yes. I'm Positive. You're my prince baby." I stopped and stared in her eyes.

"You wanna marry me Zakiya." She nodded yes and kissed me feverishly. No more words were spoken as we brought one another extreme pleasure. I washed us up and laid her in bed.

"Please don't ever cheat on me again. I won't be able to take it." She whispered laying in my arms.

"I won't. No one is worth losing you." She looked up at me.

"I definitely feel the same." We kissed and shortly after, we heard Alma yelling up the stairs that the boys were back and she's going home. I threw some clothes on and went downstairs.

I had my son and Jackson go upstairs to shower and get ready for bed. It took them a minute to finish and when they did, lil Con came in the room. Zakiya had fallen asleep and I was watching TV.

"What up man? You ok?" I made sure the covers were over Zakiya. She loved sleeping naked.

"Thank you, dad." I sat up.

"For?"

"For finding me a mom." He hugged me.

"Honestly, you found her."

"I'm happy she's going to be my mom now." He hopped on the bed gently and kissed her cheek.

"Is she going to have babies?" He asked scooting off the bed.

"One day."

"Soon dad. I wanna be a big brother." I laughed and walked him to his room.

"Good night son." I helped him in the bed and kissed his forehead.

I left and checked on Jackson in the room next door. He must've been tired because he was knocked out. I double checked the front door and went in my room. I laid back down and felt Zakiya scoot closer.

"You gonna give me some babies?" I whispered in her ear and kissed her. She stirred a little. I thought it was going to be hard but being with one-woman ain't so bad after all.

CHAPTER 11
Zakiya

"Ok. You can sign here and here." Brock told me and pointed.

"You look sexy as hell." Consequence whispered in my ear.

He asked me to dress up because we were going to celebrate afterwards. He took me to the mall yesterday and I picked out a wraparound dress and some beautiful Dior heels and a purse to match. I'm not into name brand items because I've never been able to afford them. However; if he wants to buy them, then who am I to say no?

"Thanks babe." He ran his finger down the cleavage part and stopped at the scar.

"Even with this, you're still beautiful." He kissed it.

I appreciated him even more for reminding me that the scar doesn't define me. I've never claimed to be better than anyone or pretended to be. I don't think I'm ugly either and each day he reminds me, makes me feel better about myself.

"One more and you'll be Consequence Jr.'s mother." I smiled and waited for him to flip the pages. He pointed, I signed and that was it.

"Congratulations Zakiya. You are now the mother of lil Con." He gave me a hug and Consequence cleared his throat.

"Be quiet babe. I only want you. Plus, his wife is very nice." I hugged his wife Gina as well, who came along.

I met them the second week I stayed with Consequence because once my son asked me to be his mom, Consequence jumped right on it. She's very nice and has her own gyn practice. I wouldn't say Brock and he are best friends, but they are tight as hell.

"We're gonna have lunch to celebrate, do you two wanna join us?" I noticed Brock smirk and Consequence had a grin on his face.

"Sure." We waited for Brock to hand in all the paperwork and stepped out the courthouse together.

On the drive over, I asked Consequence if we could do to Disneyworld. They may have gone but I've never been and to be honest, didn't care to until now. I always assumed it was for kids. Andrina told me to look up Universal because it's more for adults and what do you know? I saw all types of rides I wanted to try out.

"It's crowded babe. You think we're going to have to wait?"

This place was beautiful and by the water. It had valet parking only and it's not somewhere on the strip. The valet guys were well groomed and polite. I can't imagine how the wait staff is.

"The place is bigger inside. You'll see." He held my hand in his and stopped at the front to give his name. I knew he made reservations.

"Hello Mr. Waters. Everyone is here." The waiter said.

"Everyone?" I questioned and turned to see Brock and Gina grinning.

"What's going on?"

"SURPRISE!" I jumped.

"Congratulations sis. I'm so happy for you." Andrina said hugging me.

"What is all this?" I turned to where she pointed and saw the banner. It read, *Congratulations on being my mom.* I covered my mouth when lil Con stepped in front of me with a black box.

"What is this?" I sat in the closest chair. I gained most of my strength back, but I didn't wanna overdo it either.

"Open it." I did and gasped right along with everyone else. It was a beautiful locket and there were diamonds on top of the heart.

"Daddy said, you deserve it." I lifted it and opened the locket. There was a photo of me and lil Con we took one day at my house before the shooting.

"But, how did you?" Consequence stood there smiling.

"Look. Daddy made mine in a dog tag." He showed me his. I started crying and hugged him tight.

"Thank you baby. As your mom, I'm going to be the best I can be for you." I hugged him again.

"I got you this." I looked up at his mom and smiled. I haven't seen her, but she's called to check on me a lot.

"You didn't have to." She handed me a Tiffany's bag. I opened it and the box, only to find a platinum bracelet with a charm attached. It read; *survivor.*

"I need some air." I hopped up and ran outside. My breathing was increasing, and I started having an anxiety attack or something.

"Take slow breaths Zakiya." I nodded hearing Consequence voice.

"I know it's overwhelming you. You have to relax." His hands went around my waist and I felt his chin on top of my head.

"This is so nice babe. I've never had anyone do nice things like this for me." He turned me around.

"More reason as to why you deserve this and so much more." He lifted my head.

"We love you Zakiya."

"Is she ok?" His mom yelled from the door.

"Yea. We'll be right in." She went back inside.

"If I don't say it later, thank you for loving me. You took a chance on this hood chick and regardless of how many times we bumped heads, you loved me anyway."

"You're worth loving Zakiya. Don't let anyone tell you different." I nodded and allowed him to kiss me.

"Let's finish so we can go to Universal."'

"We're going?" I was excited.

"Tomorrow." He held my hands and took me inside.

"Mom, this is for you too." Lil Con approached me right at the door.

Everyone was sitting and ordering with the waiters at this point. Consequence led us over to a quiet area where only three chairs were. We could see everyone, but you had to walk over to speak. He walked off to order our food separately. He didn't want ours to get mixed up with everyone else's.

"Open it mommy." He handed me a small box and inside was a phone.

"Did daddy get you a new one?" He asked eating a piece of bread.

"I don't think so. Where did you get this?" I questioned. It's weird for him to bring me one gift, when there's more on the table.

"The waiter brought it in after you went outside. He thought it was left by accident."

"Oh ok. Do me a favor honey and go get aunt Drina for me."

"Ok." He did like I asked, and she walked over with Rock. They both gave me a hug.

"Congratulations cuz."

"Thanks."

"What's wrong?" I showed them the phone.

"Why he get you a new phone?" Drina asked.

"He didn't. My son said the waiter brought it when I ran outside. He wasn't sure why it didn't come in with the gifts."

"I don't understand." Drina said turning it on.

"The only thing I can think of is, Lisa or Conscience sent it."

"I can vouch for Conscience and tell you; she didn't send it. Matter of fact, she offered to buy you something and I declined for you." He shrugged.

"Thanks, cuz. It could only be from Lisa then." I would never accept a gift from Conscience.

Consequence told me about her coming to his job and apologizing but he wasn't trying to hear it, and neither am I. She was reckless for no reason and has to be dealt with.

"What you think she sent?"

"Let me see." I put my index finger under my chin pretending to figure it out.

"Probably something showing her and Consequence messing around. You know hateful women always catch a man slipping."

"Don't open it then. Let him handle it." Just as Rock said it, Drina opened a message. We were both nosy so even if she didn't, I would have.

"Oh shit Consequence. It feels good. Right there baby." You heard moaning. I shook my head because I should've listened to Rock.

"I'm sorry sis. It's definitely him." I took the phone out her hand.

"She must've hidden the phone in her car. You see her on top and him sitting there." I shook my head.

She had the phone on one side of the car, and it showed the

seat. The camera wasn't directly on him, but you knew it was him from the side profile.

"I don't know how she did it, but she did." Drina said and Rock was shaking his head.

He told me how the bitch watched him and Conscience have sex, so I shouldn't be surprised by this.

"Why though? Who has this kind of time on her hands?"

"Evidently she does." Rock said and walked over to Consequence. I tossed the phone on the table and a notification popped up.

"Sis, there's a message." Drina looked at it.

"What does it say?"

"Nothing." She attempted to turn it off, but I stopped her. I opened it and let the tears run down my face staring at the time stamp. It was the same day his sister shot me.

Lisa: *You laid up in the hospital and I'm fucking your so-called man. I told you, he'd never leave me alone."* There was a middle finger emoji after the message.

"I thought he was at the hospital the entire time."

"He was. She must've gone to see him Zakiya." I shook my head.

"Before you go off, I do know he was there. I told you, no one could get on the floor."

"No one could get on the floor but calling her there to fuck is just as bad." Consequence turned to me and stormed in my direction.

"Uh oh." Drina joked.

"Fix your face Zakiya." He barked, took a seat next to me and pulled me closer.

"Look at me." He turned my face.

"I don't know what she sent you and right now, I don't care. You have a son and I'm not going to allow you to be upset."

"But..."

"But nothing. We'll deal with it at home." He wiped my face.

"This is what she wants Zakiya."

"He's right sis. I don't know how she found out about today, but she did. This is to hurt you; to make you leave. Don't let her win Zakiya. You know where's he's been every day and night." I had to agree. It wasn't a second of the day, I didn't know where he was.

"You're not weak Zakiya. You're strong and beautiful. You're the woman I picked to mother my son and the woman I'm going to marry and grow old with one day." I snapped my neck.

"Yes. I am going to marry you one day, and I gave you a promise not to ever cheat on you and I won't." He held my face in his hands.

"Baby, I need you to show everyone how strong you are. Don't allow the bitch to break us. We worked hard to build what we have just for her to try and make it crumble." I nodded.

"I swear that whatever she sent, I'll look at later and handle it. This is your day babe. You and your sons'. Get it together. You got this." He kissed my lips.

"You got this Zakiya." Drina squeezed my hand.

"You're right. She can't break me. I got my man, my sister, my family and my son."

"That's right. Now fuck her and let's enjoy the rest of the day." Drina said and hugged me tight. She went to sit with Courage.

"I'm gonna fix this babe."

"Please do. I don't want your indiscretions coming out at every event you have."

"They won't." He kissed me again and we enjoyed the rest of the day with our family.

The video stayed on my mind, but I didn't dwell on it. He will have to answer questions when we leave; that's for damn sure.

CHAPTER 12

Andrina

"You sure about this?" I asked Zakiya. We were sitting outside Lisa job waiting for her to get off.

The day after she adopted lil Con, they went to Universal for a week. They came home late last night and now here we are.

"Not really." Was her response. I started the car to leave.

"Wait! There she is." She pointed to Lisa going to her car speaking on the phone.

She's a pretty woman. I'm talking model type and had the body too match. I felt like Zakiya looked better than her but when your man continues sleeping with someone from his past, you know it goes past looks.

"Follow her." I pulled out slow and stayed two cars behind her. She has no clue what I drive; yet, I didn't wanna make our presence known either.

"What the fuck?" Zakiya shouted as Lisa parked in front of

this huge house. Shit, it appeared to be a mansion. There was no gate and the landscaping is gorgeous. Two other cars sat in the driveway along with a regular bike.

"No wonder the bitch has a bad body. She probably bike rides the area." Zakiya said making us both laugh.

"What you wanna do?" I asked because Lisa went in the house already.

"I'm going in."

"Bitch, we going in." She looked at me.

"I told you before, y'all have a whole soap opera dialogue going on and I ain't missing shit." She smacked my arm and we stepped out.

"How much you wanna bet, Consequence pays for this?" She said as we looked around.

"No. You think so?"

"The bitch works at the hospital. Ain't no way her salary can afford this; unless she running it, which I doubt. The bitch don't seem to bright."

"I remember Courage mentioning her working in radiology or something." I asked him what she did for a living since she had so much time on her hands.

"Yea. He definitely paying for this." I agreed and followed her to the door.

DING! DONG! It took her a few minutes to answer. She got the shock of her life when her eyes laid upon us.

"What the fuck you want?" Lisa snapped.

"Move bitch." Zakiya pushed past her and this time, we got the shock of our life.

"Nice isn't it?" She joked as I glanced around and noticed her place to be an exact replica of Consequence house; well him and Zakiya's.

"I have to make it feel like home when he's here." She smirked and folded her arms across her chest.

"Has he seen this?" Zakiya asked still observing the place.

"Chile please. Plenty of times." She walked off and switched in front of us.

"Let me call you back Ciara." Lisa said out loud trying to get a reaction outta me.

It didn't matter because both of us were walking around her house like we friends with her.

"What you want?" Zakiya headed upstairs ignoring her.

"You have got to be kidding me?" We stopped at the first bedroom.

"What?"

"Bitch, this is the bedroom set Consequence has." I turned my face up. Not only does she have too much time on her hand, the bitch is clearly obsessed.

"I told you. He had to feel like home here. How's the bed in his place Zakiya? Does he fuck you and make you grab the canopy pole while he hits it from the back?"

"What is it you want Lisa? You said he won't leave you alone; married or not so what's the problem?" Zakiya questioned.

"After your dumb ass got shot and he left the hospital, he won't answer my calls, or text messages. I tried to go to his job, and they threw me out."

"Shouldn't it tell you something?" Zakiya said she was ready to go. We went down the steps and to the front door.

"It tells me he may stop funding my lifestyle and I can't have that." Both of us froze. I know she didn't just say what I think she said.

"Excuse me."

"Excuse you what?"

"He pays for this?" She tossed her head back laughing.

"Pay? No. He purchased this and my cars. He pays all my bills and set me up with a hefty bank account that he replenishes monthly."

"Anything to keep the side chick quiet." Zakiya whispered and I heard her.

"Call me what you want but we both know if he didn't want to be with me, he wouldn't. Now like I was saying..." She was about to talk shit. I noticed Zakiya breathing heavy.

"I hate to ask you this, but can you get her some water?" I held Zakiya's hand in mine.

The shooting had taken such a toll on her, that when she gets excited or upset, it affects her breathing. Here we are months later and when this happens, it feels like it went down yesterday.

"Breathe Zakiya. I told you we shouldn't have come here."

"I had to see why she's stalking him." She was bent over with her hands on her knees.

"What the hell taking her so long?" Just as I said it, she sashayed back with a water bottle in hand. I popped the top and handed it to Zakiya.

"Get your ass the fuck out my house before you die." Lisa snapped making both of us stare. I couldn't stop Zakiya's reaction if I wanted to. She started beating the hell outta Lisa.

"Zakiya that's enough. Come on." I finally pulled her off when Lisa stopped fighting. I snatched her hand and walked out to my car.

"You ok?"

"I don't know. My head is dizzy and..." She vomited on the ground.

"Let's get you home."

"Take me to your place. I'm not going there." She began dry heaving and instead of taking her to my place, I drove to the hospital. They took her right in.

* * *

Three hours later, the two of us were on our way to my house; well Courage's. He told me to say it's mine but sometimes it felt funny.

"She good?" Courage asked helping her walk.

"The doctor said she ingested bleach."

"Bleach?"

"Exactly. He didn't have to pump it because it was a small dose. I think Lisa put it in the water bottle."

"Lisa? What the fuck going on? You said, y'all were out and she felt dizzy. I knew, I should've sent someone to watch you."

"Not right now." We took her in one of the guest bedrooms

and laid her down. I put the covers on her and he snatched me out the room.

"Tell me right now what the fuck happened before I call him." He had my back against the wall. I had to stop myself from grinning at how sexy he looked angry.

"You ain't getting no dick so you may as well tell me."

"First of all, I am getting dick because that's my shit." I removed my shirt and bra to turn him on and it worked.

"Whatever." He took his shirt off.

"Anyway..." In between him carrying me up the stairs and stripping each other of clothes, I gave him a short rundown.

"Put it in baby." He locked the bedroom door.

"Why should I? Y'all had no business..."

"Ssssss Courage." I moaned out as he entered me.

"No business going over there." He placed his hands on the bed, on each side of my face and stared down; not missing a stroke.

"You ready to be a mom again?" I never let him cum in me because I was scared of getting pregnant and losing it again.

"I'm not a mom Courage."

"You may have lost the baby, but you were a mom." He rammed in harder.

"Now let me ask again. You ready to be a mom?"

"Baby." I dug my nails deeper in his arms.

"Baby nothing. You owe me for pulling this bullshit. My brother about to be pissed." He went harder.

"Ok Courage. Yes. We can have a baby." He lifted my legs on his shoulder and penetrated me harder.

"I was putting one in you regardless." His lips found mine and for the next hour and a half we did a lot of nasty things. He exploded in me twice and I heard him whisper in my ear, he hopes I'm pregnant. I rolled over and dosed off with him behind me.

CHAPTER 13

Courage

"Tha fuck you mean you're not coming home?" I heard Consequence barking downstairs. I looked at the clock and it read seven. Drina and I slept the whole afternoon away.

I slid outta bed, used the bathroom, handled my hygiene and put clothes on. If my brother going off about her not coming home, I wonder if he knows why? Not that it's my business but I told him to get rid of Lisa. She's a pain in the ass and it's only gonna get worse.

"Bring my son here." Zakiya had her arms folded leaning on the wall as I made my way down the stairs.

"He's staying at my moms and why the fuck aren't you coming home?" I closed the front door he left open.

"You think I wanna sleep in a house that looks exactly like hers?"

"Like whose?" I shook my head. Even I knew she was speaking of Lisa.

"Lisa. The bitch house is an exact replica of yours." He was quiet for a few seconds. Probably thinking of what to say.

"How did you see her house?"

"I went over there."

"For what?"

"Because Consequence, I wanted to know why she keeps fucking with me."

"I told you I'd handle it." She laughed.

"Handle it how? By taking away the house and cars you brought her, not paying her bills or giving her monthly deposits?"

"Oh shit." I said out loud by accident.

"Yea she told me everything and my question is, why are you taking care of her?" Zakiya was pissed.

"It's complicated."

"Ain't shit complicated. The way I see it is, you wanna keep your side chick around so if we don't work out, she'll be there. She's the only loyal one to you. It's how you feel right?" Zakiya snapped and he didn't respond.

"You know what? I don't wanna argue. Can you bring my son to me tomorrow?"

"Zakiya." He reached out and she snatched away.

"I'm not staying in a house she's duplicated her own with, and I'm not staying with a man who can't leave his side chick alone. Nope! I won't do it."

"Bet." He stormed out the house and she retreated back to

the other room. I looked up and Drina was leaning on the banister shaking her head.

"You hungry?" I asked.

"Yea."

"A'ight. I'm going to pick something up from my sister restaurant. Text me what she wants." She nodded and I grabbed my keys. I needed a break from all this and it ain't even my shit.

* * *

"Listen Courage, I don't mind watching my grand baby but I'm too old for this." Ciara's mom said on the phone. I was on my way back with the food and she called.

"My son there?" I asked and made a U-turn when she answered yes. I didn't think to call Drina because my anger was building, and I didn't wanna snap on her.

I parked in front of Ciara's mom house and jumped out. This isn't the first time the bitch has done this since he's been born. She must think she's hurting me by going out. I could care less. The only problem I have is her using her mother. She's in her fifties and has health problems of her own. She doesn't need to cater to a child at her age.

All Ciara is doing is, making me hate her more for being a bitter baby mama. The things she's said about Andrina are hateful and ignorant. My girl has never done anything to her and I damn sure didn't cheat on Ciara, with Andrina. I didn't even know her when we were together.

"Hey Courage. I'm sorry to bother you." She opened the screen.

"It's never a bother to take care of my son." I walked in and found him in the swing I had put over here. I was under the assumption my son would be here sometimes; not almost everyday.

"I don't know what's wrong with her. One minute she's loving him and the next, she's calling for me to watch him." I shook my head.

"Let's go man." I picked him up and grabbed his baby bag and car seat.

"Tell Ciara don't bring her ass to my crib. I'll bring him home when I'm ready."

"Be careful with your girlfriend Courage." Her grand-mother said as I put the seatbelt on my son.

"What you mean?"

"I hear Ciara speaking on how much she hates her and..." I cut her off.

"Andrina hasn't done anything to Ciara. To be honest, my girl is the one who told me not to kick Ciara out the house. She has no reason to hate her."

I told Drina how I paid for everything Ciara had; including the house and car. At first, she didn't agree with me continuing to pay but because she had my kid, it wasn't fair to make my child live in other conditions when his father had money.

Therefore; I allowed Ciara to stay even after she cursed me out a million times for not being with her. And now her grand-mother telling me I need to watch my girl. I never underestimate any woman so I will take heed to her warning.

"Have a good night." I kissed her cheek and watched her go in before pulling off.

When we got to the house, I noticed Andrina sitting in the front with Zakiya. Those two are thick as thieves. It's funny how both of them are in love with brothers who had a reckless ass sister. I don't know what I would've done had Conscience shot Andrina.

"Hey babe. Why is he here?" She asked taking him out my arms.

"His mother disappeared again."

"A damn shame." She walked ahead of me. I put the food down inside and sat with Zakiya on the porch.

"Why can't he leave her alone?" She asked with her head back.

"He has." She looked at me.

"I'm serious. He stopped all contact with her, blocked her from everything and she's not allowed in his office building or anything he owns."

"Then why is he paying her bills?"

"I can't answer that. I thought he stopped." I shrugged and lit the blunt I had rolled before leaving.

"I know they have history but damn."

"As you know, Consequence has a hard time committing." She nodded.

"Lisa has been around for a very long time and she's friends with my sister." She sucked her teeth.

"He has love for Lisa, but he doesn't want her."

"Do you know the crazy bitch has every piece of furniture Consequence has?" She shook her head.

"I can believe it. She obsessed with him."

"Sexually, I can see why if he's done her the way he does me." She joked.

"TMI Zakiya." She laughed.

"Consequence is a great man." I gave her the side eye.

"He was rough in the beginning but after breaking down his walls, I got to know the real him. He's everything I want in a man; except for his smart-ass mouth and arrogant ways."

"I'm sorry to tell you this, but no matter how long you're with him, that ain't ever going to change."

"I don't want it to because he makes me laugh." I shook my head.

"You're angry right now and I get it. I wouldn't be comfortable staying anywhere Drina lived knowing her ex had his place set up the same."

"At least you understand." I took a pull.

"He understands too." She turned her head towards me.

"You'll be surprised. Consequence may not say it, but he heard you loud and clear." I told her.

"I hope so because I miss him already." She said good night and went in. I sent a message to my brother telling him to come get his woman. He said, she can stay where she at. Those two are definitely made for each other.

I finished smoking and went inside to see Andrina burping my son. I locked the door and asked if she ate.

"I will when he's asleep." He burped and she took him upstairs to bathe. By the time she finished, he was asleep, and I brought her food in the room.

"Thanks babe. Can you turn the monitor on?" We had one in the room for when he stayed over.

"When you're done, let's hop in the jacuzzi." She looked up chewing.

"You read my mind." I laughed and shortly after, the two of us had fun in the jacuzzi.

CHAPTER 14

Lisa

"Bitch, you keep playing with Courage." I shook my head at Ciara as she sat across from me.

Ciara told me how she dropped her son off at his fathers because she wanted to make him stay in the house, as if he cares. If he ain't working or doing whatever else, he's up under his girl. Denial is her best friend.

We were at the club getting drunk. I didn't wanna come out because the Zakiya bitch gave me a black eye and a busted lip. My head and nose hurt a little but otherwise I'm good. I give it to the bitch; she got some hands on her.

I never thought she'd come to my house though. I enjoyed her facial expression as she observed my place. I don't know why she mad; I told her Consequence loved feeling like he's home. He did call me all types of crazy bitches when he first seen the furniture though.

Eventually, he got used to it because it didn't stop him from coming over. I wonder if the bitch died after drinking the bleach I put in her water bottle. People should know by now not to ever drink from someone you don't like.

Shit, I emptied some of the water out, grabbed the bleach from under my sink and poured it in. I couldn't do too much because it would've turned white. I tightened the cap, rinsed the bottle under the water in case it smelled, dried it off and handed it to her. I know she drank it; I'm just wondering if she died.

Anyway, Ciara is a beast at makeup, and you can't tell I had a fight at all. She did the damn thing when it came to covering it up. I guess she would with all the niggas she fucking and the hickeys she had to hide. She just happened to luck up and get pregnant by Courage.

It's crazy because she was in love with him but didn't wanna be bothered because he was always handling business outta state and the country. Then, he gets a woman and she stopped sleeping with whoever and got pregnant.

I'm in love with his brother too but she doing too much. I hope he doesn't take the baby and leave her with nothing. The way she carrying on, I won't be surprised if he does.

"He ain't doing shit. What's going on with you and Consequence?" She dismissed my statement.

"You know how we do."

"How do we do?" I turned to see Consequence standing there looking sexy.

He had on denim jeans with a jersey and some all black Jordan's. His hair always made you seasick with the waves and he made my heart melt whenever he smiled.

I lifted myself out the seat and stood in front of him. His cologne invaded my nostrils like always and his presence alone made my heart skip a beat.

"How do we do Lisa?"

"What are you doing here?" I ignored his question.

"Tryna figure out why you keep fucking with my girl." I waved him off. He caught my wrist and bent it back so far, one wrong move and it'll snap.

"Consequence. Please you're hurting me."

"And you keep hurting my girl with the childish shit you doing." He barked.

"I'm sorry." I tried to move his hand, but the grip became tighter.

"I think you're ready to go." He let go and I hit the ground.

"Ron, get this bitch and let's go." Ron snatched me up by the back of my neck and pushed me out the door. People were staring; yet, not one person intervened. Ciara attempted to say something, and Consequence shut her down.

"My car is here." I said and he ignored me. Ron put me in a black truck and Consequence sat in the back with me.

"Lisa, how long have we known one another?" He asked pulling out his phone.

"Since we were fourteen. What's this about?" I continued rubbing my wrist.

"This is about how I let you control me for years."

"Consequence, I never controlled you." He laughed.

"I thought the same thing until my girl made me realize, it's exactly what you've done all these years." I sucked my teeth.

"All the women I've slept with, you've managed to slither your way in to make sure, I didn't form a real relationship with them. That's until Lauren came around and saw right through you. Granted, I managed to creep with you even after marriage knowing it was wrong." He shook his head and stared out the window.

"We didn't have sex but sucking me off was still bad."

"Consequence." I touched his arm and I thought he was going to kill me.

"After finding out she cheated, what did I do? I came right back to you." Inside I was smiling because no matter who he was with, he always came home.

"Oh, there were still other women, but you were loyal. You never turned your back on me and dropped anything to be with me."

"I love you Consequence. I always have and always will."

"I know and that's a problem."

"Why is that?"

"Because you never took the time out to look elsewhere. You knew I'd always return." I smirked.

"It worked until now."

"What?"

"Zakiya Summers is my woman and may be my wife one day." He turned his head to look at me.

"I'm not gonna do the same thing to her, I did to Lauren because she's better than both of you in every way possible." I sucked my teeth.

"You sent her a video of me fucking you the day she got

hurt. That was good Lisa, but you forgot one thing." He gave me a devious grin.

"You forgot Zakiya isn't weak. She's not gonna allow you to run her off with your bullshit; only proving to me more and more as to why she deserves to be my wife without me dipping out."

"I'm not worried Consequence. Your dick loves me so whether you marry her or not, I'll still be around." He threw his head back laughing.

"Not this time Lisa. You see, Zakiya got a nigga hooked, strung out, and ready to kill for her." Ron reached in the glove compartment and passed him a gun.

"I'm not ashamed at all to say she's got the best pussy I've ever had. Shit, I feel like a bitch sometimes from the way she has me moaning." He put bullets inside.

"You're good too Lisa ain't no mistaken that. However; she's better and no one will come before her but my kids." I didn't say a word.

"The crazy thing is, you've always been ok being second in my life no matter what." I should probably feel offended by his words but I'm not. This is the position I chose to be in.

"I'm at a point now, where I can only handle one woman and Zakiya is that woman." He took the safety off.

"This is your one lifeline Lisa." The truck stopped.

"Where are we? This isn't my house." He chuckled.

"Oh, the house I paid for, along with the cars. All that shit is gone." He put the phone in his pocket.

"Huh?"

"You heard me correctly. As of this very second, you're homeless. You own nothing, your bank account empty and any credit cards you had are cancelled. The clothes, purses, shoes and everything else in that house is going to charity."

"What am I supposed to do?" The door opened and Ron stood there.

"This is something you should've thought about before opening your mouth to my girl. I mean, it was a matter of time before I took it all anyway. However; you sped the process up." He stepped out and walked around to where I stood.

"Strip."

"Excuse me." Ron leaned on the truck.

"You heard me. Strip."

"Consequence." He aimed the gun at my head, and I removed my clothes quickly.

"Everything you have on, I most likely purchased." He's right. I used the money he put in my account.

"The bra and panties too." I took them off and he tossed them in a bag Ron handed him. He set the bag on fire; basically, telling me I can't even wear them to leave.

"You got one more time to send my girl anything or talk shit to her and I'm gonna kill you." I tried covering my body with my hands.

"And to show you I'm not playing, here's a *leave me the fuck alone* gift." He put the gun in his waist and Ron handed him something else. It was dark so I couldn't be positive, but it appeared to be a knife.

"I didn't correct a lotta shit you did in the past and I blame myself. But what you won't do is ruin anything I'm building with Zakiya." He walked me over to a tree and put my hand on it.

"AHHHHHH!" The knife went straight through. My hand was literally stuck to the tree with the knife still in it.

"Have a good night." He hopped in the truck and left me there naked and bleeding. What the fuck is wrong with him?

CHAPTER 15

Conscience

"How was the party?" I asked my mom. I came over to see both of my nephews. Lil Con was upstairs playing the game as usual. Her and my father were excited to have more grandkids and had them over a lot.

"Very nice. I mean she had a moment from being overwhelmed; otherwise she enjoyed herself." I nodded.

"You and Rock back together, I see." She lifted Courage son up to change."

"Yea. I'm happy too." I burped my son who just ate. He's so greedy and Rock has me putting a little oatmeal and rice in his bottle to fill him up. Talking about he's a boy and they eat a lot.

"Good. I hope you learned a lesson from all of this." I felt a lecture coming on.

"I did and I apologized to Consequence as I'm sure you know."

"Mmm hmm." She mumbled.

"He's not accepting it and..."

"And what? You think he should and move on right?" She pulled my nephews pants up and went to throw the soiled diaper away. I heard her washing her hands and once she stepped back in the room, I knew it was a therapy session from her. As bad as I wanted to leave, I couldn't because she'd curse me out.

"I didn't say that ma. I'm trying to right my wrong and he doesn't wanna hear it."

"Would you wanna hear anything he had to say if he shot Rock?" I put my head down.

"Listen Conscience, this is not about to be a drawn out lecture because we've discussed your reckless behavior already. You need to understand the seriousness of all this."

"I do ma."

"Do you because the way I'm taking it is, you're trying to apologize, and no one is listening. You want things to return back to normal because you said sorry and they're not having it. Let me explain why." She started feeding lil Courage. Yup, both of my brothers named their first sons after them.

"Rock told you countless times he wasn't cheating and instead of believing him, you have him followed, only to lead you straight to his cousin, in whom you almost killed." I cringed listening to her say it.

"Had you listened to your man and not some bitter woman who wanted you to dwell in misery the same as her, it would've never happened." I remained quiet.

"Lastly, you stole that woman's spirit when you shot her,

and I think it's what's killing your brother the most." I looked at her.

"He loved the way Zakiya challenged him. She was about her shit. She didn't need or want a man for anything. It's what drew him closer to her. But you did what you did and now she's dependent on him and even though she won't say it; he notices it." I felt like shit because I had no idea Zakiya was going through it the way she's describing.

"She won't ask him for money because her pride won't allow it, but she does say what's needed in the house and whatever lil Con needs." My mom held my hand.

"She legally adopted your nephew and can't spend money on her own son because she's outta work. There's no billion-dollar bank account she saved up for rainy days Conscience. You took everything from her and that's why your brother won't forgive you." I felt my eyes becoming watery.

"I know you're thinking, Consequence can give her whatever she needs but do you know he still has yet to tell her who he is?"

"He thinks she'll want him for his money." I said.

"That's one reason. The other is, he hasn't told her because she hadn't asked." I gave her a strange look.

"She's aware he owns a few clubs but that's it. Actually, I think it makes him feel better that she hasn't asked, because it shows him, no matter how much money he makes, it has nothing to do with her love."

"I don't know what else to do or say." I let the tears escape my eyes.

"It's nothing for you to do, except leave it alone. Your brother will speak when he's ready and not a minute too soon." I wiped my eyes.

"Have you handled the situation with Lisa?" She asked. I hadn't seen or heard from her since Rock caught her watching. I guess it's time to handle it. I asked if she were ok keeping an eye on all three kids and she yelled at me. I kissed her cheek and went to speak with Lisa.

* * *

"Did Lisa move?" I questioned myself in the car. I pulled up to her front door, stepped out and rang the doorbell.

After a few more times of ringing it, I peeked in the window and it was empty. No furniture or sign of life anywhere. I walked around over to the garage and it too was empty. I called my father.

"Is everything ok Conscience?" I heard concern in his voice.

"Yes daddy. I was just wondering if Consequence mentioned Lisa moving. I came by to discuss what she did and there's no one here." He laughed.

"Did she move? No. Did he throw her out? Yes." I gasped. Never in a million years did I think he would get rid of her. Maybe Zakiya is having an effect on him.

"When?" I went to my car and stopped when I noticed a black SUV driving past slowly.

"Last week." I stood there waiting to see if someone would get out.

"Conscience." My dad yelled in the phone. He was telling me something; yet, I wasn't paying attention.

"I'm here dad. Does he have someone watching the place?"

"No why?"

"Someone in a black SUV just drove by really slow." I told him and remained calm so whoever is in the truck didn't think I noticed them.

"Get outta there Conscience." I placed him on speaker and hopped in my car.

"What's going on?" I asked driving down the street.

"Someone is tryna kill your brother or should I say, is after him."

"What? Who? Courage or Consequence?" I questioned driving and checking my mirrors.

"Consequence."

"For what?"

"That's the answer we all wanna know. He handled the guy who tried to take my grandson but before he died, he told Consequence the person said he has something he wants. Before you ask, we have no idea what it is."

"Consequence doesn't even bother anyone unless necessary. Neither does Courage." Regardless, of what's taken place, I'll never wish anything bad on my siblings or anyone they're with. I fucked up with Zakiya and I'm owning up to my shit. I won't let anyone fuck with her either.

"I know and it's why Consequence is worried because

Zakiya won't go back to her place since the shooting. Not that he wants her too but if someone is after him, he doesn't want them showing up at the house where her and lil Con are."

"I understand." I grabbed the gun out my purse and laid it on my lap just in case.

"Where are you now?"

"At the light on... oh shit..." I yelled seeing the black truck coming full force at me.

"What happened Conscience?"

BAM! The entire side of my car was smashed. My head hit the window and dazed the hell outta me. I quickly opened my door and stepped out.

"Are you ok ma'am?" I heard voices but my only concern was getting the person in the truck who hit me.

BOOM! BOOM! I let my nine-millimeter do the talking until the bullets ran out. I hit the windshield and door.

When I finished, I opened the other persons door and pulled the guy outta the truck the best I could. The lower half of his body was still in being his legs were pinned under the steering wheel.

"Who the fuck are you?" I asked myself because he was dead from the bullet in his head.

"Ma'am are you ok?" Someone else asked and I felt my head getting dizzy.

"I need to sit." I asked to borrow a lady's phone and dialed up Rock.

"Yo!"

"Babe, I need you."

"Conscience? Where are you? Why are you calling me from an unknown number?"

"I was being chased and the truck ran into me." I heard sirens and saw EMT's pulling up.

"What? Where are you?" I gave him the address and told him to meet me at the hospital.

CHAPTER 16

Rock

"What up?" Consequence answered.

"Something happened to your sister." He was quiet for a minute.

"Someone was chasing her and ran into her." I told him since he didn't ask. He may not care for her, but he doesn't want her dead either.

"Where is she?"

"I'm on my way to the hospital now."

"Was my nephew there?"

"I don't know. I'll hit you up when I get there." He hung up and I didn't even bother contacting anyone else. I'm sure he will.

I rushed inside the ER asking questions. The receptionist led me in the back, and I saw Conscience on a stretcher. The tech was asking her questions and heading in another direction.

"You ok?" I grabbed her hand when the tech stopped in front of the X-ray department.

"I think so. I hit my head pretty hard and... hold on." She sat up.

"Is that Lisa?" She pointed to a woman who had a pair of scrubs on.

"I don't know. Finish telling me."

"I need to talk to her."

"After you tell me what happened." She nodded and informed me of how she stopped by to confront Lisa and a truck drove slow by the house, and eventually followed her; crashing into her car. She killed him and now she's here about to get an MRI of her head.

"Rock? Conscience? What happened to you?" Lisa asked coming closer. I saw the anger on my girls face and just as Lisa got close, Conscience jumped off the stretcher and started wailing on her. Lisa had no win whatsoever.

"That's enough Conscience. Get on the stretcher." I glanced around and it was only one other worker and an older woman sitting in the waiting room. You could tell Conscience was dizzy because she almost lost her balance getting back on.

Some worker ran over and asked if Lisa needed help or wanted her to contact the police.

"No. I'm good." Lisa knew what it was.

"You sure because..."

"She said no bitch. Move the fuck on." I barked and the woman went to sit behind the desk.

"What is the problem Conscience?" She grabbed tissue to

stop her nose from bleeding. Why she didn't walk away is beyond me.

"Let's go Miss Waters. Lisa you ok?" The tech asked. Conscience had fucked her up. She probably should go home.

"I'm ok." He took my girl in the back and said it's going to take over an hour because they were a little backed up and MRI's take time. I went to use my phone and heard Lisa calling my name.

"What?"

"Why is she upset with me?"

"Did you really just ask me that?" I shook my head.

"I didn't do anything."

"Watching us fuck isn't doing anything?" I sent out text messages to my team for them to find out who's responsible for my girls' accident. Lisa walked away and into a bathroom.

"Hey ma." I answered. She was expecting to have the baby tonight so I could take Conscience out. She still enjoyed date night and so did I.

"What time you bringing the baby over?" I started to fill her in, when Lisa emerged from the bathroom and headed in my direction. Blood stained the front of her scrubs and specks were on the pants.

"Let me call you back ma?" I disconnected the call when she stood in front of me.

"Look. I'm sorry. I stopped by the house and saw your car there. I figured you two were talking and stayed outside for a few minutes." This is true. When she arrived, she sat in the car from what the security camera showed.

"When I realized you weren't coming out, I knocked, and she didn't answer. It didn't dawn on me to use the doorbell, so I looked through the window thinking she had the earphones on." I stared down at her. Conscience did wear earphones in her ear but never loud enough where she couldn't hear our son cry.

"I noticed you two were... Umm..."

"Fucking. We were fucking." I said it for her.

"Yea and I watched."

"Why? She's supposed to be your friend. Tha fuck is wrong with you?" She shrugged.

"You were fucking the shit outta her and I watched. So what? I didn't know you liked her to lick under your dick."

"Bitch." My hands were around her throat.

"Get off me." Her nails were scratching the top of my hands.

"Yo. Let go Rock." I heard Courage's voice behind me.

"Nah man. This bitch gotta lot of mouth." He pulled me off. Her body hit the floor and she tried hard to catch her breath. I got down to her level and looked her straight in the eye.

"Don't fuck with me bitch. I'll kill you in this hospital." I kicked her hard as hell in the stomach.

"You crazy man." Courage said laughing.

"The bitch stood outside your sister house watching us fuck."

"What?" Now he was mad. Lisa got up and hauled ass the best she could outta there.

"Is she ok? What happened?" Their mom ran in with my

son while lil Con and Courage was behind her with their father.

"Someone crashed into her."

"Why?" Her mom asked.

"I don't know. I have people on it now trying to find out who's behind it." I plopped down in one of the chairs. One by one, they each did the same.

"Consequence?" We heard Conscience say as the tech walked her from the radiology department. We turned to see him walking up on the phone.

"What did they say?" He asked staring at his mom.

"She just came out."

"You ready son?" He asked lil Con who ran over to him.

"Where's mommy?"

"At uncle Rage house."

"When is she coming home? I love uncle Rage but mommy misses being at our house." All of us looked at Consequence who ran his hand over his head. I was aware of their quarrel because my mom filled me in.

"I know. Daddy had to make some moves first." Consequence moved by his parents and kissed both of his nephews on the forehead.

"Ok. I'm staying over there tonight." Consequence shook his head and the two of them left. I walked over to Conscience still on the stretcher.

"I have to wait on the results, and we can go." She said and I kissed her.

"Give him time Conscience."

"It's been a long time." I shook my head at her.

"You weren't the one affected. He's with her every day and sees the struggle she goes through. Just be happy he showed up." She nodded and left it alone.

The tech pushed her back to the ER and an hour later, we left. She had some bruising on her side, but her head is fine. I took her to my house and told her she's only to go to her parents' house until we find out what's going on. She can be mad all she wants. Her safety is my only concern right now and finding out who did this to her.

CHAPTER 17

Zakiya

"Daddy said he's making moves for you to come home. What's taking so long?" Lil Con asked me.

"What is he talking about?" I asked Consequence who was standing in front of Rage's fridge drinking a soda.

"I don't know."

"My aunty was in a car accident mommy." I lifted my head. Consequence shrugged.

"Ok. Can you bring this to aunty Drina?" I handed him the baby wipes I originally came downstairs for. The baby was here again because Ciara trifling self-dropped him off and bounced.

"What's he talking about?"

"Somebody crashed into her car tryna kill her." He shrugged again.

"Consequence it's ok for you to care in front of me. She's

your sister and I'm nobody." He slammed the soda down and yoked me up.

"You are somebody Zakiya that's why I can't fuck with her right now."

"Stop it." He had my shirt balled up.

"She did a number on you and I hate to see you second guessing yourself. I want the old Zakiya back. The one who wouldn't tell me to let go of her clothes, but the one who would push me off and curse me out. Where is she?"

"She's gone Consequence and I doubt she's coming back." He let go.

"I'm so scared to behave the same in front of you because I can't protect myself."

"Zakiya."

"I'm weak now. I can't even play fight with you because I lose my breath too fast. Consequence, I wanna dig deep within myself and be who I used to be, but I can't." Tears just started racing down my face.

"I haven't left this house since I been here because I have nothing to leave for. No money, no car, no place to live. NOTHING!" I shouted.

"You have no idea how it feels to have nothing." I push past him and walked outside. I didn't want my son to witness me this upset when I've been so strong in his eyes.

"What do you need to get better? Tell me what to do and I promise, I'll get it done before tomorrow." He rubbed my shoulders.

"I don't know. Can I borrow like five thousand dollars to get me a new place with furniture and...?"

"I'll give you the money for whatever you want but it damn sure won't be to leave." I turned around.

"Consequence you're very well established, and I have not one dime to my name." I never saved money because I barely made any. What I did have, went to bills, food, utilities and clothes.

"Why do you want someone who can't match your fly or do anything for you? I couldn't do anything before but at least I could buy you a card, take you to the movies and then dinner. Now all I can do is make you dinner with the food you buy and find a good movie on Netflix or amazon prime with the bill you pay."

"Come here." He wrapped his arms around me, and I cried harder. My body was shaking, and it felt like it was taking me forever to calm down. I think this is the first time I really broke down about my well-being.

"Look at me." He moved me back and used his thumbs to wipe my eyes.

"Whatever you need, I got you."

"Consequence."

"You want money in the bank? Done. You want a brand-new house? Where do you want it built? You want a new wardrobe? I'll send a stylist over to get your sizes. Whatever you want baby, I swear I got you. Just don't give up on yourself; on us. We need you." He rested his forehead on mine and then our lips touched.

"If we not about to fuck or you giving me head, then this has to stop." I chuckled and wiped the rest of the tears.

"I'm sorry for breaking down. I love you and lil Con. Sitting around makes me feel worthless. I know Rage doesn't mind but it's not me." He grabbed my hand and led us in the house.

"DRINA!" He shouted and she came to the top of the stairs.

"Lil Con is going to say here while I take Zakiya out."

"Ok. Set the alarm when you leave." He nodded and we walked out and to his car.

"I miss you doing this." I referred to him opening the car door.

"You've been here almost a month; you missed a lot." I rested my head on the seat and relaxed. He held my hand in his as we drove. I really missed him.

* * *

"What are we doing here?" I asked when he pulled up to the house. It's still beautiful as ever.

"I wanna show you something." I waited for him to open the door and followed him.

"If you don't wanna stay after being here it's fine. I wanted you to know, I heard you." He unlocked the door and my mouth hit the ground.

The whole downstairs had been completely changed, all the way down to the floors. They used to be wooden like and now they're marble. The furniture used to be gray and now it's black and white to match the floors. The kitchen had been remodeled and the dining room too had a makeover.

"Come on." He carried me upstairs and not only did he change the master bedroom into a different room, he knocked down a wall to make it bigger and the bedroom set was different and so was the color.

"You like it?" I felt like a crybaby because all I could do is cry staring at the pictures from my house lining the walls of a small office right outside the room. It held a desk with a computer, small TV and loveseat. The little name plate said *Zakiya, Lady Boss*.

"What... why..." The words wouldn't come out right.

"You were right about staying in a place, Lisa had resembling this. It wasn't fair to you and I wouldn't want you uncomfortable in your own house. You wanted changes and I had them done."

"The office?" I pointed.

"You said one day you'll be your own boss so; I'm going to make it possible."

"Huh?"

"Whatever you wanna be, tell me and it's done. You wanna own a hair salon, I'll make it happen. If you wanna own a limousine service, I'll buy the cars and set it up." He walked over and lifted my head.

"I know you're used to being independent and it's what I love the most about you but let me be the one to make any and all dreams you have, come true."

"Consequence."

"It's your world Zakiya. Just tell me what you want."

"The first thing I want, right now at this very moment, is for my man to make love to me all over this house."

"You sure?" He asked as I started unzipping his jeans.

"Positive. Unless he doesn't want any."

"It'll never come a time when I don't." He and I started kissing one another with so much passion, both of us could've probably cum off it alone.

His hands moved to my breast and cupped them. He caressed both and slightly pulled on my nipples. I let a low moan out he smiled. Once they were hard, his hands moved down to my belly and trailed down further. His fingers ran up and down the thin fabric of my panties.

He went slow and then fast making my pearl grow. He moved me to the bed, laid me down and removed whatever clothing I had left; leaving me completely naked. He opened my legs wide and kissed upwards. The closer he came to my treasure, the more aroused I became. I'm sure he could see and smell my sweetness seeping.

"I missed you Consequence." He said nothing.

His hands moved to my bottom lips and spread them open. He began to tease and lick which made me whimper like a child. Each time he touched my clit, he'd swipe over it with his tongue and stop. My body arched and I basically stuck my pussy in his face.

Consequence dove in touching and teasing before slipping his tongue inside. I grabbed the side of his head and grinded my pussy all over his face. If I could put him in me; I would have because it felt so good. He stuck those fingers in and brought me to ecstasy.

"YESSSSSSS! OH, GAWD YES!" I don't care how loud I was. He had my body on fire. He stood and plunged his way in my tunnel causing me to yell out again and dig deep in his arms.

"You gonna have my babies one day Zakiya." He said and all I could do is nod my head yes. His dick was so big and once he got into a rhythm, he dug deeper. The harder he penetrated, the more I cried out for him to keep going.

"Fuck me hard Consequence. It's been a month and I know you need me like I need you."

He flipped me over, spread my legs and began abusing the shit outta my pussy or should I say uterus. I was in dick heaven right now and Consequence knew because he kept hitting that spot I loved.

"God you feel good." He stopped, pulled out and laid back on the bed for me to ride him. I bounced up and down with my breasts swinging with me. He started tugging on them making my eyes roll.

"Make me cum Zakiya." He smacked my ass and it drove me insane. I stood on my feet and went faster.

"Your pussy inhaling my dick. Yea. Damn it looks good ma." He pulled my face down to his and thrusted harder. Once his finger went in my ass, I lost all control of my body.

"Got damn you sexy as fuck cumming this hard." He said and didn't stop.

"Consequence." He flipped me over again and had my legs behind my head.

"Yea."

"This pussy loves you baby. You hear her talking. She wants you to cum for her." He loved when I spoke dirty to him.

"Oh shit Zakiya. Keep talking."

"She so got damn wet for you. Mmm hmm. This your pussy. Cum for me baby. Fuck yea, you feel good. I'm cumming again. Oh God."

"Oh shit ma. I'm about to cum. Fuck."

"Go head baby. Give it to me." His lips crashed on mine.

"Mmmmm." We both groaned and let go. I wrapped my arms around his neck and felt his heartbeat racing. Neither of us moved.

"There was no way in hell, I could've pulled outta that good shit. I have to get you a pill Zakiya." He pecked my lips and pulled out slow.

"Ok." He carried me in the bathroom.

"We can work on having kids when you're my fiancé." I rested my head on his shoulder as he started the shower.

"Whatever you want." He put me down in the shower and got in with me.

"You will be my wife." I nodded and let him wash me up. All I wanted to do is go to sleep and he must've felt the same because he was right behind me.

CHAPTER 18

Consequence

"You ready man?" I asked my son who was anxious as hell.

"Yup." He grabbed the blindfold out my hand.

"Don't forget, it's a surprise."

"I know dad." He ran down the stairs and found Zakiya in the living room watching television.

Hell yea, I packed her up and brought her home. Andrina had a fit because she didn't want her to leave but too bad.

"Mommy."

"What's up baby?" He sat next to her.

"Daddy and I have a surprise for you." She smiled.

"You do? Where is it?"

"I have to take you to it." She turned around to me and I shrugged.

"Ok let's go."

"You have to wear this blindfold." She looked at me again.

"Don't look at me." She laughed and let him stand behind on the couch and put the mask on her eyes. I wanted to use a bandanna, but Rage said she'll be able to see from the bottom. My whole family knew the surprise.

"Can you see mommy?"

"No." Her hands instantly went out to feel around. I walked over and held her hand.

"Let me put your slippers on." I lifted her foot and slid them on.

"Let's go dad. We're gonna be late."

"Late? Where are we going? Consequence, I'm not dressed." She whined.

"Relax Zakiya. You worry too much."

"Fine." Lil Con and I walked her to the car and after putting her seatbelt on, I went back to make sure the front door was locked, and the alarm was on.

"Where are we going?" She asked.

"It's a surprise mommy." Lil Con spoke from the back seat. She pouted and folded her arms across her chest. I was shocked she didn't try and remove the mask.

We drove for about twenty minutes and pulled up to the strip. She had no idea where we were going which only made this better. I enjoyed seeing her smile and after today, it's all I ever wanna see from her.

"We here." My son hurriedly removed his seatbelt and jumped out the car.

"Can I lift the mask?"

"No." I said and walked around the car to open the door. I helped her out and lil Con was already gone.

"I'm going to remove it now." I stood on her side and lifted the mask. She had to adjust her eyes away from the sun.

"A jet? Did you buy me a plane?"

"Hell no. You got some banging ass pussy but I ain't buying you no plane. You bugging." She smacked me on the arm.

"Wait a damn minute. Does it say Consequence on it?"

"Yup."

"Conceited." She joked.

"You already know." I took her hand in mine and led her to the stairs. The jet was custom made with two bedrooms and two showers. My mom did most of the decorating though.

When you first stepped on, it was made like a lounge area with two long couches and two loveseats. It held a small kitchen area and mini bar. There were two televisions in this area and one in each bedroom. I wanted it to have a home type of feeling and it does.

"Mr. Waters." The captain tilted his hat.

"Hi." Zakiya spoke to him and I made her walk in front of me. The shorts she had on lounging around the house were short. I didn't give her the chance to change.

"What is this?" She stepped on and looked around.

"Since you love eating Italian food, it's only right we eat it from its original place." She turned around.

"We're going to Milan." I told her. I owned quite a bit of businesses and property over there as well.

"As in Milan, Italy?" I nodded and she gasped.

"Consequence, I don't have any clothes and..." I shushed her with my finger and pointed to the back.

"Oh my God!" She yelled digging in the bags from Prada, Gucci and Dior.

"Babe, this is too much." She stared at the platinum diamond necklace and earrings hanging on the mannequin head. They were ocean blue tear drops with the tear drop necklace to match.

"I didn't want them to take it off and had it brought over just like that."

"I don't have anything glamorous to wear with it." I went in the closet and took out the black dress bag and unzipped it.

"Consequence this is beautiful." She removed the dress from the bag and laid it on the bed.

It was a sky-blue strapless dress with diamonds lining the top. There was a split on both sides leading all the way up to her thigh, damn near exposing her pussy. I passed her the silver, open toed shoes the stylist matched with it, along with the clutch.

"But my hair and nails aren't done."

"That's where I come in." A woman who works at the hotel stepped on. She worked in the spa and did mani and pedis. Her husband does business with me, which is why he's getting on too.

"Hey missy." Gina said stepping on with Brock and their son.

"Oh my goodness. Are we all going?" I shook my head yes.

"Can y'all give us a minute?" Zakiya asked and walked to

the back of the jet.

"Mr. Waters, now that everyone is onboard, we'll be pulling out." I nodded and went to where Zakiya was.

"What's wrong?" I asked and she closed the door.

"Nothing." She literally rushed to get my pants down and swallowed me so fast, I couldn't stop her if I wanted to. I bit down on my lip and gripped the shit outta her hair just to keep the moan from escaping my mouth. It didn't take long at all for her to make me succumb.

"This is the exact reason you can have anything you want." She stood and wiped her mouth.

"Why because I give you good head?"

"Nah, because not only do you give good head, you got my heart." I put her hand on it and she started crying.

"You've had mine for a while now." We started kissing until my son knocked on the door. She ran in the bathroom to clean her mouth.

"Where's mommy?"

"In the bathroom." He stepped in the room and jumped on the bed.

"You sleepy?" Zakiya asked after walking out.

"No. I wanted to see what you were doing." I chuckled, kissed her and walked in the front with everyone else.

* * *

"We'll be landing in five minutes." The captain said over the intercom.

It would be 7pm when we got there, and our reservations are at 8. The restaurant is twenty minutes from the air strip and a limo is waiting.

For the last two hours, each of us showered, and got dressed. We weren't going to have time when we arrived, which is why I had towels, washcloths, soap, toothpaste, toothbrushes and all necessities needed to get ready on the jet.

"We have arrived." The captain said and Brock knocked on the room door to let the women know we were here. Of course, it took them forever to get ready.

"Ok. We'll be right out." Gina peeked out to say.

We stepped off the jet and waited at the bottom for the women. There was a cool breeze and I hoped it wouldn't rain because it would mess up my plans.

"We're ready." I looked up and the first two ladies came down and then her. I took a deep breath watching Zakiya walk down the stairs with lil Con. Amazing, can't even explain how beautiful she is. I felt my heart racing with each step she took.

"You better do right by her or I swear, we'll find a way to kill you." Gina sassed and made her way to Brock. I met Zakiya at the bottom of the steps.

"You look beautiful babe." I pecked her lips and led her to the limo.

"You sharp son."

"I know." He ran off with Gina and Brock's son.

"If I don't say thank you before the night is over. Thank you." She said and carefully got in the limo. The driver closed the door and we were on our way.

CHAPTER 19

Zakiya

I held onto Consequence hand on the drive to wherever our reservations were. He still hasn't told me what's going on but who cares? I'm in Milan, Italy. Home of the fashion designers and fashion shows. *I wonder if they're any going on while we here.*

The limo stopped in front of this huge building. It seemed vacant; yet, there were other exotic cars out here. Consequence grabbed my hand and waited for everyone to step out.

"Zakiya, before we leave this limo, I need to know you're ten toes down for any and everything." I placed both hands on the side of his face to make sure I had his attention.

"I'm ten toes down, ten fingers down and my whole body and spirit down too."

"That's all I need to hear. Let's do this." He helped me out and walked closer.

"This is the Sforzesco Castle. It holds a lot of art treasures from what they say." He gave me a quick rundown of this beautiful building.

"It's huge." I said looking around.

"It's supposed to be closed but I know people, who know people, and had it opened for us." I swung my head towards him.

"What? How did you do that?" He smiled and led me down a short tunnel that opened at the end.

"Consequence." I covered my mouth staring at the candlelit tables set up, along with a small band playing. There were tables upon tables of food and the red carpet made me feel like a princess.

"Bitchhhhhh, Courage better do some shit like this for me or we over." Drina joked pulling me in for a hug.

"When did you get here?"

"This morning. He wanted to have sex in Italy first and then go shopping." Consequence sucked his teeth.

"Girl, this city is beautiful. I can't wait until tomorrow when we can go out together."

"Bye Drina." He shooed her away. She gave him the finger and went to where her seat is.

"Mr. Waters. Miss Summers." The waiter spoke as he pulled out my chair.

"Would you like a glass of wine?" He asked me.

"Sure."

"I didn't know what you liked so I ordered five different brands." Four other waiters came over and stood next to him.

"This is The Chianti Classico, the Barbers D'asti, the

Langhe Nebbioli, the Poggio Badiola and the Tenuta delle Terre Nere." Consequence spoke with an accent and it turned me on.

"They all sound so expensive."

"Don't worry. They're not." I sucked my teeth.

"What? They're not. I wasn't sure if you drank wine and I wasn't wasting money on it." I ignored him and pointed to one of the bottles. The guy poured it and before I could sip it, lil Con ran over.

"Is it time dad?"

"Not yet. I'll get you when it is."

"Ok." He ran over to the other table. I never got the chance to see who's here because the way the tables are set up, each one is private.

What I mean is, the tables had these small canopy's over top with curtains. If you wanted to close them, you could and let's just say, some weren't open; including where I saw Drina sitting.

"Hey Miss Zakiya." Alma spoke and gave me a hug. I guess she's here to watch lil Con.

"I'm going to get us a plate." Consequence said and left me sitting there with her.

"How are you?" I asked.

"I'm good. Are you happy?"

"I am and it's not even my birthday." She smiled.

"He loves you Zakiya." She rubbed my arm.

"I love him too." I smiled as he spoke to my cousin who I now know is here. He waved but didn't come speak. That's weird.

"Good. When are we getting some more babies to run around the house after?"

"I have no idea." She and I both laughed.

"Enjoy the food. It's great." She kissed my cheek and walked away when he sat down.

Throughout dinner, I noticed Consequence checking his phone a lot. I refused to ask questions in case whoever it was, aggravated him. I didn't want him upset with me and ruin the evening.

"Let's dance." I wiped my mouth, threw some lip gloss on and followed him to the dance floor. The band began to play slow music which is appropriate for how he and I were dancing.

"You know you're beautiful?" I had my arms on his neck.

"I know because my man tells me everyday." He kissed the side of my neck.

"I'm going to continue telling you as long as you live."

"Well since you said that, I should tell you, you're very handsome."

"I've been told." I shook my head.

"It's only believable coming from your lips tho." He leaned down to kiss me.

"Can I ask you something?" He stared in my eyes for a few seconds, then looked away to call Lil Con.

"About time." He said and stood next to his dad. The music stopped and everyone stared. I didn't know why until I turned around.

"Oh my God!" I gasped and covered my mouth seeing Consequence and lil Con on their knees.

"Zakiya, you barged in my life at a time when love wasn't even a thought. To be honest, you irked my nerves and I wanted to kill you many times." I wanted to respond but the words wouldn't come out.

"Then you saved my son and I'll always be in debt to you for that. It brought us closer and the best part is my son gained a mother; a real one. You're helping me raise him to be a young man and he loves you. I want you to know that I will do anything to keep you in my life. Will you marry me?" He opened up a box holding a gigantic pink ring.

"Yes baby. Yes." I barely got the words out before he placed the ring on and scooped me up in his arms. I could hear applauds behind me.

"Wait, it's my turn daddy." Lil Con yelled and it became quiet.

"I'm sorry man. Go ahead." He pulled out a piece of paper.

"I didn't know you when I was born but I know you now. I'm glad you're my mom and marrying my dad. Please don't ever leave us. I love you mommy." He dropped the paper and pulled a small box out his pocket.

"This is my ring to you. It goes on the other finger." It was another diamond but not as big as the one Consequence gave me.

"I love you son and I'm not going anywhere." I kneeled down and hugged him tightly.

"Ok mom. I wanna play. I love you." He kissed my cheek and ran off.

"Damn ho. Two men asked you to be in their life and I only have him." Drina joked and pointed to Rage who laughed.

"Congratulations sis. I'm so happy for you." We hugged and right after, I noticed everyone there because we were being congratulated all night.

By the time we made it to hotel, it was after two. Alma would not let us keep lil Con in the room. She said, we needed to consummate our engagement.

His parents refused to keep any of the kids as well. They said it's been a while since they've been on vacation and needed to explore one another. Consequence was mad as hell.

"Are you happy Zakiya?" Consequence asked coming closer as I stood outside the villa naked and in a sheer robe.

We each had separate villas which were a mile and half away from one another. They couldn't see us, and we couldn't see them.

"I'm very happy. I wouldn't want this with anyone but you." He turned me around and placed his body behind mine.

"I never thought I'd love another woman but here you are with the key to my heart."

"And it's mine forever. I'm not gonna hurt you baby." I know he still has doubts because of what Lauren did but I'm not her.

"Show me what my future wife can do on this beach." I sipped the rest of the wine and sat the glass on the table.

"Come then." I removed the robe and made love to my

fiancé out in the open. Any fantasy I wanted with him sexually, he let me do or he did it to me. I was in my glory and no one could take it from me.

"You stuck for life Zakiya." He wrapped his arms around my waist in bed.

"So are you." I turned over to kiss him and we fell asleep holding one another.

CHAPTER 20

Andrina

"Where is my son?" I heard Ciara barking at Alma when she opened the door.

Crazy as it sounds, Alma's the nanny for all the Waters grandchildren. If all of us went out at the same time, she'd keep them with her, or their parents would. They're a pretty close-knit family; well, up until the mess Conscience did. Courage speaks to her every now and then, but nothing like before.

I think what she did hit him hard because of the miscarriage and Consequence. He was devastated by it; I lost our child and yet all she did is apologize and get upset because no one wanted to hear it.

Anyway, we arrived from Italy early yesterday morning and as soon as we stepped foot off the jet, her mother called saying the baby was there and needed him picked up. She had a doctor's appointment and couldn't take him.

"Courage is not here Ciara." Alma spoke calmly to her.

Allegedly, she gets very nasty at times. I haven't witnessed it yet; but at the rate Ciara is going, I'd say today it may happen.

"I'm not here for him. Where is my son?" Aggravation and anger spilled from her mouth and I knew the time was coming for this bitch to bug out. I sat lil Courage in the swing, buckled him in and put my slippers on.

"Like I said..."

WHAP! I heard and saw Alma's face turn sideways. Not only is this woman in her late sixties, she ain't no fighter. Why in the hell would Ciara lay hands on her?

"Move bitch." She barged past Alma and stopped dead in her tracks after seeing me.

"How can I help you?" I questioned placing my hair in a ponytail while she stood there staring me up and down.

I had on a pair of shorts with a T-shirt and slippers on my feet. Even though it may not appear to be fancy, in her eyes she had to have assumed differently, because she looked me up and down and sucked her teeth.

"I'm taking my son." I stood directly in front of her.

"The son you're barely around? The son Courage has to pick up from your mothers house all the time?"

"None of your business ho."

"Ho? I'm far from that and you know it. It's the reason I'm living here and you're not."

I gave her the same hateful stare she just gave me.

"Who fucks all types of men and gets angry when the one

she trapped on purpose with a baby; is how you put it, right?" I reminded her of what she said to me before.

"He doesn't want you Ciara." She rolled her eyes.

"Oh, I forgot, you're his ride or die chick? Yet, you leaving your son wherever, just so you can go out thinking it's going to piss him off. I'm sorry to tell ya, but the only pussy he's worried about is this one right here." I pointed to myself. She was beyond mad at this point, and I loved every minute of it.

"Whatever." She tried to bombard her way past and I caught her by the hair and watched her body drop. I yanked it so hard; she fell backwards.

"First of all, don't bring your ass in my house disrespecting Alma or myself."

"Get off my hair." She tried to pry my hands off and failed. I drug her to the door kicking and screaming with my hand gripping the hell outta her hair.

"Apologize to Alma."

"No." She was still trying to remove my hands.

"Apologize now." She refused and after seeing Alma standing there visibly upset and crying, I lost it on her.

POW! I punched her in the face over and over until I felt my body being lifted.

"You good?" Courage asked examining my face.

"Get this bitch outta here and if your guards allow her to past them one more time; you and I are gonna have a got damn problem."

"What?"

"You heard me. You were supposed to handle that when she stopped by in labor."

"Oh shit. I forgot man."

"Yea well since you forgot, the bitch came over and attacked Alma and..." I didn't get a chance to finish because he literally drug Ciara out by the feet and down the driveway the same way. She was screaming and I have no doubt, the entire back of her was scraped up.

"Did she punch or smack you? Your face is swelling up." I stared at Alma standing there in shock. I guess she couldn't believe what Courage did.

"You know he doesn't play when it comes to me." She nodded.

"Let's get you some ice." She followed me in the kitchen.

I smiled at my stepson who had no idea what happened. He was engaged in the television and at his age, he wouldn't know what he was looking at anyway.

SLAM! The door shut and I heard Courage's feet stomping up the stairs.

"Let me check on him." She grabbed my hand.

"Thank you Andrina."

"Anytime." I left her sitting there and made my way upstairs. When I stepped in the room, Courage was removing his clothes.

"What happened?" I started explaining and his facial expression spoke volumes.

"Babe, don't do anything drastic." He turned before walking in the bathroom.

"You don't want me to do anything drastic but you talking shit about her popping up and I understand. But did you stop to think that we had so much going on, I forgot?"

"I know Courage and I apologize for snapping."

"It's never ok for you to attack your man in front of another bitch." He went to shower, and I sat on the bed thinking about what took place.

I snapped in front of Ciara which probably made her think we had issues. Shit, for a minute, I thought he didn't want to make the change. I went in, stripped and apologized sexually until we both got tired.

"Hold up. You telling me the bitch stopped by unannounced demanding her son and hooked off on Alma?" Zakiya couldn't believe it. I stopped by her office and told her what happened.

Yea, we still worked at the hotel. Consequence made her take the job back just so she'd have her own money and I wasn't letting Courage dictate my finances. I never had to ask for money but having your own makes you feel independent. It may not be as much as what they have, but it's ours.

"Yup and the ho thought she could beat me. You should've seen me Zakiya, I was whooping her ass. I let out all the anger from losing the baby, my parents, the breakup and just everything." I felt myself becoming upset.

"Awww it's ok. At least you beat her ass."

"I did. She had it coming." I lifted the top off the soda she handed me.

"Sooooo, how does it feel to be engaged?" I lifted her hand and stared at the big ring.

"Good. Lil Con is really happy. You know he said the colors for the wedding should be navy blue since he looks good in that color?" We busted out laughing.

"He is his fathers child." She said shaking her head.

"Do you know how much the ring cost?" It was beautiful. She stared down at it and smiled.

"I don't know."

"Well bitch. I overheard Courage discussing it on the phone with his brother the night he proposed. He asked how much it cost and girl." I had to take another sip of soda.

"What?"

"Evidently the ring is the largest Flawless Fancy Vivid Diamond ever made. The diamond has 59.60 carats in it and is the most expensive ring in the world."

"What?"

"Bitch, you won't believe what it cost because I couldn't believe it myself until I looked it up." I pulled my phone out and searched *most expensive diamond in the world* and showed her the ring.

"Oh my God!" She covered her mouth.

"71.2 million dollars for this? Is he crazy? Wait! I mean how can he even afford it?"

"I said the same thing, so being the nosy person I am, I

searched up the Waters family and almost lost my breath." I showed her the page with them on it.

"250 BILLION DOLLARS!" She shouted and snatched the phone out my hand to make sure she wasn't seeing things.

"I think its split between them but still. They're each worth billions on their own."

"They're billionaires?" She said again not believing her eyes. It's basically the same thing I did when I first found out.

"I was shocked too because they don't even act like it."

"That's why Ciara had the baby." She said and handed me back the phone.

"Remember when she said, she trapped that billionaire dick and we laughed it off as her saying it's what it felt like?"

"Oh shit." I forgot she said that, and it never dawned on me to look them up until Consequence mentioned to Courage how much it was.

"Sis, they own a lot of shit all over the world and in other countries. They even own one of the damn oil companies in Saudi Arabia." I told her after putting my phone down.

"These people aren't rich Zakiya; they're rich, rich. Like they could just bathe in money or throw it in the ocean and still be rich." Both of us shook our heads.

"I can't believe he spent all that money on my ring."

"It's money well spent and if you wanted another one; I'd get that too." Consequence scared the shit outta us.

"Babe. This was too much. I could've taken a ring from Jared's." She took it off and handed it to him.

"Get your money back and then we can shop for a cheaper one." His facial expression changed.

"Don't ever in your got damn life take this ring off again." He snatched her hand and forced it on her finger.

"Consequence."

"It could've cost a hundred million dollars and I would've still gotten it for you."

"I just thought..." He cut her off.

"Don't worry about what I do with my money."

"Consequence it's no need to get angry." She tried to calm him down.

"I'm just gonna go." I tried to ease out before he snapped on me.

"Bye and don't come over here again upsetting my fiancé. Why would you even tell her? Messy as fuck." Guess not.

"I'm sorry. I thought you told her." He turned to me.

"What nigga you know is gonna tell his fiancé how much the ring cost he proposed with?"

"True but..."

"But nothing. Bounce." I jumped and walked backwards out the door.

"You don't have to yell." Zakiya said which made him turn his head back to her.

"Call me later so I know he didn't kill you." I joked and hauled ass. I was off anyway.

Maybe I should've kept my mouth shut but he needs to blame Courage. No one told him to have Consequence on speaker. If he didn't, I would've never known.

CHAPTER 21

Zakiya

I woke up this morning on a mission. A mission to make my man speak to me. It's been a week and he hasn't said anything to me besides, he'll see me after work. I understand he's upset I found out about the price of the ring and offered to downgrade, but he's flat out being petty.

I dropped lil Con off at his grandparents and drove to Consequence job. This will be the first time I've been there since we've gotten together. I stayed away because he always seemed busy and I didn't wanna be a distraction.

I pulled up at a gigantic glass building with security everywhere. They were at each exit of the many parking lots. A post sat in front of the building and I even saw two guards walking the area. I guess billionaires need this type of security.

"Hi. My name is..." The security guy cut me off.

"Zakiya Summers." He answered.

"How do you know my name?"

"I ran the license plate and it gave me all your information."

"That fast?"

"No need to waste time. Here." He handed me a ticket.

"Put this in your windshield and park in lot 1."

"You don't even know why I'm here." He stepped outside the post and in front of my door.

"Miss Summers, there are fifty floors in this building and thirty of them have businesses on them. The other twenty hold offices and conference rooms. Do you really believe I'm going to ask everyone here what's their purpose?"

"Ugh. I guess you have a point."

"I told you to park in lot 1 because someone just left, and most women arrive in heels. Lucky for you, it won't be a long walk."

"Thank you."

"When you get out the car, walk through those gates and the front entrance will be on the right."

"Ok." I went to pull off and he stopped me.

"You'll need your ID and an officer will screen you through a metal detector."

"Well damn."

"Mr. Waters is very strict with his businesses and buildings. He makes sure every environment is safe for his employees and visitors."

"That's good to know. But how are you safe?" He smirked.

"You have no idea who our boss is. All I can say is, no one feels threatened here." He winked and told me to pull in. Another vehicle was behind me.

I parked, grabbed my purse and phone and headed in.

"How are you today?" The female security guard asked as she searched my purse and sent me through the detector.

"I'm good. Thank you." I retrieved my belongings out the bucket it falls into from the conveyor belt and started to the front desk.

My mouth damn near hit the floor just by looking at the lobby. There were fountains with statues, lounge chairs, a small bar and eatery. In another spot held a newspaper stand that sold candy, and other things like that as well. I stopped in the coffee shop and even this place was nice. I ordered and went to the elevators.

"Ma'am. You need to sign in." The receptionist said.

"Oh. I'm sorry. This is my first time here and I've been in awe of it all." She smiled.

"It happens to everyone. How can I help you?"

"I'm here to see Mr. Waters."

"Do you have a meeting?"

"No. I'm..."

"Zakiya." I turned to see Brock coming in a different door.

"Hey. I was coming to surprise Consequence."

"He's gonna be surprised alright." I put my hands on my hips.

"She can come with me." He told the secretary and had me walk with him. The elevator opened and he had to use a card just for it to move.

"Why is he going to be surprised? It better not be a woman here?" He chuckled.

"I see why you and my wife get along. Woman, no one is even allowed on his floor but me, his family, his secretary and now his fiancé."

"Oh." He lifted my hand and examined the ring as if he didn't already see it.

"He told me you found out about the price of the ring."

"I tried to have him return it."

"Let me give you some advice on Consequence." I sipped the Macchiato I purchased from the coffee shop.

"He doesn't trust anyone but me and his family."

"I know."

"He's the way he is, because all the women he's dealt with have only wanted him for his money; even Lauren."

"What? And what floor is he on?" He laughed. We were passing the 32nd one. I didn't pay any mind on what he pressed because on this elevator, you input the floor and it disappears. Maybe it's to keep others from knowing where you're going.

"He's at the very top."

"Should've known." We both laughed.

"Anyway, you're the first woman who had no idea who he was or how much money he made, and he loved it."

"Why?"

"He wanted you to want him for who he was as a person and not what he could give you."

"He is definitely hard to deal with but that's why I love him. He gives me a run for my money and believe it or not, I see a different side of him. The vulnerable and peaceful side."

"Exactly and it's why he fell harder for you. It took him

forever to open up to Lauren and when he did, she fucked up. With you, he's seen you at your highest point and lowest." I put my head down.

"You adopted his son, became his fiancé and moved in with him. All he wants to do now is give you whatever you want, no matter what the cost." He pointed to my ring when the elevator door opened.

"Don't take away the special moments he has for you."

"I won't do it again." I felt even worse after hearing that.

"Trust me when I say, he loves to make you happy." We walked past the secretary without speaking and down a long hallway. I could see his office straight through the glass. His back was turned as he stared at the computer.

KNOCK! KNOCK!

"I have a surprise for you." Brock said and Consequence turned around with a flat expression.

"I'll take it from here." I told him and closed the door once he left.

I sat my cup on the mini bar because he had a glass desk and I didn't wanna leave a stain. I placed my purse and phone on one of the chairs.

"What are you doing here?" He leaned back in his chair.

"I'm sorry for removing the ring from my finger and offering to return it. It was a gift from your heart, and it shouldn't matter how much it cost." I looked behind me to make sure no one was coming and straddled him in the chair.

"I won't take it off again." I pecked his lips and sucked on his neck. It's one of his spots and his manhood twitched.

"Whatever I do for you is because I want to." He lifted me off his lap, stood and walked over to the door.

"Your friend is nosy as fuck." I let a grin creep on my face when he locked the door.

"She is but I'm not going to lie and say if your brother did the same, and I overheard the conversation, that I wouldn't mention it, because I would." He shook his head.

"Press the button on the side of my chair." I looked down and did like he asked.

"What the hell?" These navy blue blinds began to come from the top of the glass windows and the door. No one could see in or out.

"What else did you come here for?" He asked removing the button-down shirt and tie.

"Nothing."

"Yea ok." He tossed his things on the chair.

"I know your period went off yesterday and you're horny." He kicked his shoes off and slid his pants down.

"Consequence, I only came by to..." He lifted me out the chair and removed every piece of my clothes.

"You came to get fucked because you know as well as I, we're addicted to each other." He kneeled down in front of me and took a whiff of my scent.

"I see your juices slowing coming down and I haven't even touched you." He moved me to the window, pulled the chair over to sit and lifted one of my legs.

"Dammit." Once his tongue slid in between my folds, that was it. I exploded three times before he stopped.

"I want my dick sucked but after you cum all over it." He pulled my body to his and mounted me.

"I think it's time to put my son or daughter in you and there's no more swallowing, pulling out or using plan b pills." He slammed me down so hard, I had to stop him for a minute.

"You ok?"

"Yea. I think you just shifted my uterus and scrambled my Fallopian tubes." He busted out laughing.

"I'm sorry. Your pussy so fucking good, I go crazy when I'm in it." He moved me slow in circles and the two of us stared at one another. It's like, we not only became lost, but we showed through our eyes how in love we were.

"I love you so much Consequence and I promise to never hurt you." He smiled.

"Same here Zakiya. Can I put my seed in you?" He pulled my face close to his and our tongues became lovers. I pumped harder on top still not breaking the kiss. The sex became more aggressive and animalistic.

"Fuck Zakiya. You're about to make me cum quick." I went faster.

"It's ok. I know the second round will be longer. Put your baby in me." His fingertips dug deeper in my ass cheeks.

"Yea baby. It feels good. Don't stop." I moaned when he thrusted under me.

"I'm ready Za. You ready?"

"Yes. Give it to me." He nodded and stuck his finger in my ass. My entire body began to convulse and shake. He held me tight as he released every seed he could inside.

"Let's get married tomorrow." I breathlessly said with my head on his shoulder.

"Good dick will make you say anything." He ran his fingers up and down my back.

"It will but I meant it." I lifted my head and kissed him.

"I don't need a big wedding Consequence. I just wanna be your wife. Our family will be complete when I have your last name."

"You serious?"

"Yes. If you want me to sign a prenup; I will. Just don't add not being around lil Con in there." He stared at me.

"I don't want your money, businesses, houses, cars, nothing. Just you and lil Con." I put my hands on the side of his face.

"You're like a dream come true Consequence."

"And so are you." I slowly lifted myself off and chuckled as his limp dick slid out.

"What you about to do?"

"My fiancé mentioned having his dick sucked with my cum all over it. I think there's no time like the present." I saw him smirk and gave him some of the sloppiest head ever. Today was a good day.

CHAPTER 22

Lisa

"I can't believe he stabbed you." Ciara said walking around my small apartment.

The night Consequence took me from the bar and stripped me of everything, I went to her house. Someone was driving by, rescued me and brought me to the hospital where I had to receive over fifty stitches. I also lost full movement in my hand and my tendons are messed up. I never underestimated Consequence, but I didn't think he'd harm me either.

Verbally, he's always been nasty to me and I never said a word. It's who he is, and I accepted him for that. He's never laid a hand on me until now. What did Zakiya do to make him hurt me?

Anyway, Ciara and I were never the best of friends, but we were cool on the strength of Consequence and Courage. We've been plenty of places together and when they had business meetings, we'd hang out.

The place Rage purchased for her is just as big as the one Consequence had for me. She said I could stay as long as I wanted but no thanks. I wanted my own because I knew he would come back eventually, and I didn't want him here.

I only stayed with Ciara until I made enough to save up for a security deposit for first months' rent. Once I did, I went straight to Walmart and purchased an air mattress to sleep on and odds and ends. I made decent money and applied for overtime which helped me get furniture and whatever else I wanted. It's not a big place but it's mine and no one can take it from me.

Ciara cool as hell but the only thing I don't agree with is how she's handling her son. I've witnessed her leaving the baby crying in the crib because she didn't wanna be bothered. A few times, I had to get him and either he was wet or hungry. I'm all for trapping a man but not with a baby. Nothing wrong with having children; however, I'm not birthing one just to keep a man. Especially, when I enjoy my freedom.

Even now, Ciara drops the baby off to her mom and I don't think I've ever seen her cuddle or even love on the child like most moms do when they first have one. It's been a few months now and he's stayed with her mom and his father more than anything.

Even tonight, we're going out and her son is not at home. She can sit in denial all she wants but I have no doubt in my mind that Rage will indeed take him away.

"I don't think about it anymore." I said staring down at the scar. As bad as I wanted something bad to happen to him for what he did, I quickly tossed the thoughts out my head.

"If I were you, I'd..." She started to say, and I cut her off.

"Don't Ciara."

"What?"

"If I even thought about touching Zakiya, he'd kill me and I'm not ready to die."

"Me either bitch. I'm just saying." She stopped to apply lipstick.

"We need to let those bitches know; those are our men." I shook my head. She truly believes Rage won't harm her and usually I'd agree. But since he's been with his girl, he isn't playing no games.

"Let's go girl. You talking crazy and if you're gonna die tryna get a man who doesn't want you, at least get tore up first." We laughed and gathered our things to leave.

* * *

"Damn it's packed in here tonight." I shouted as we finally stepped in the club. The line was long as usual and sadly, Consequence isn't my go-to guy anymore and this is one of Courage's club in South Beach. I chose not to go to one of his, in case he's out.

I thought security wasn't going to let us in, this one but he paid us no mind.

"Hell yea bitch. Let's find us some ballers tonight." She laughed as we sashayed through the crowd to get in the bathroom. Standing outside made me feel like I needed to check myself over.

"Thank you." I said to a woman who held the door for me.

"Girl, just that fast, I saw two men who looked like they were balling." Ciara said making me laugh. It was cut short when both of those bitches stepped out the stalls.

Jealousy was written all over my face as I stared at the Prada heels and expensive looking outfit the bitch wore. The purse matched as well but nothing prepared me for the humongous pink ring on her finger. I've never seen one so big. It was beautiful. All it did was bring my hatred for her to the forefront.

"Well look who it is?" Ciara started and both of them sucked their teeth as they washed their hands.

"What can I do for you Ciara?" The woman Andrina said drying hers.

"You can back off my man and..." She tossed her head back laughing as Zakiya shook her head.

"Your man? Ciara when are you gonna bring yourself outta denial?"

"Ain't nobody in denial but you. I told you from the very beginning, I'm his ride or die

and ain't shit changed." She moved closer to Andrina.

"Everything changed when he tasted this pussy."

"What the fuck eva. When I'm ready to take him back, be prepared to move out." She laughed again making Zakiya do the same. It burned me up to see this bitch living my life.

"Let's go sis. These bitches obviously have too much time on their hands." They went to walk by and besides hating on

Zakiya, I noticed how slow she moved. I took this as an opportunity to step in front of her and say some things.

"You think he's gonna stop messing with me because he gave you a ring?" She turned around.

"Excuse me." A woman said walking in between us.

"I know you're upset he still hasn't chosen to wife you up." The bitch spoke with a smile on her face. I'm about to hurt her feelings real fast.

"What?" I snapped.

"It's the reason jealousy fell from your face the second you laid eyes on me."

"Not at all." I tried to speak, and she cut me off.

"I have never bothered you Lisa and to this day, it's all you do when you see me. Now I understand you were removed from your home and no longer drive the vehicles you once had. Who do you think is responsible for that?" She smiled and folded her arms.

"When he was with Lauren, Consequence risked his marriage holding on to the loyal mistress. But I'm here to tell you, that he won't risk anything with me. It's why I have this ring and you don't."

"Oh shit." I heard Ciara say. She backed off Andrina quick, probably assuming the girl would fight her again.

The day she stopped by my house; I couldn't believe the way she looked. Her entire backside was scraped up and her face looked like the elephant man. Andrina whooped her ass and Courage did her dirty dragging her down the concrete. Zakiya did me bad but nothing like Ciara.

"He gave you a ring like he gave Lauren, and..—? It means nothing because he'll come back."

"You are a delusional woman." She turned to leave.

"And truth be told, we all know he's only marrying you because his sister almost killed you." The bitch froze.

"LISA!" Ciara shouted.

"Fuck her. The bitch thinks she better than me." I stared at how watery her eyes were getting.

"Hmmm. Did I hit a nerve?" Her body swung around.

"The hood talks boo. Evidently, Conscience assumed you were sleeping with Rock and put the bullet in your chest."

"Who the fuck told you that?"

"One... I work in the hospital and don't forget, while you were fighting for your life, I was riding Consequence's big ass dick." I saw her fists balling up.

"Two... it's a shame you didn't die."

"Don't do it Zakiya." Her friend pulled her away.

"So go head first into that guiltless marriage." I stepped in her face not caring if were about to fight or not.

"Each time y'all fuck, and wake up to one another, just know had his sister not shot you, you'd be another bitch he's fucking for a while before tossing her out." I looked her up and down.

"I may have been the loyal side chick or mistress like you say but boo remember, I had that dick for years. Whether you wanna admit it or not, he definitely has feelings for me." I smirked and headed to the door.

“Now sit your ass in denial bitch.” I walked out feeling good about what went down.

“Bitch that’s fucked up.” Ciara said walking next to me.

“She thinks she’s better than me, so I took her right off that high horse.”

“We gotta go.” She grabbed my arm.

“Why?” I questioned.

“That’s why?” She pointed to the top floor and there stood Consequence and Courage. Zakiya and Andrina hadn’t made it to them yet.

“Yea it’s best. The bitch is probably gonna cry and he’ll be mad at me.” The two of us left and partied at a hole in the wall. Fuck all of them.

CHAPTER 23

Courage

"What the hell took you so long in the bathroom? I was about to come in there." I grabbed Drina's hand and pulled her in front of me.

"Consequence, can we go?" Zakiya asked making me look at my woman.

"It's only midnight. You sure?"

"Yes." He lifted her head.

"What's wrong?"

"Nothing. I'm tired and..."

"Try lying to someone else. What's wrong?" She started crying and we both looked at Drina.

"The last time I said something, you told me off Consequence. You have to wait for her to say it." I laughed because she told me how he blasted her for looking up the ring and mentioning it to Zakiya.

"Wipe your face before we leave." She used the back of her hand.

"When we get home, you're going to tell me the truth." Zakiya nodded. We all walked down the steps and through the crowd.

"Boss, I'm sorry. I didn't know she came in." One of the guards said to me as we walked out the door. Consequence and Zakiya kept going.

"Who?" Drina squeezed my hand.

"Ciara."

"Ciara?" I questioned.

"Yea. I had to make sure the count was right after getting money out the registers. I didn't know until they walked out."

On packed nights, I'd make him clear the registers every hour and count the money for me. He'd put it in the manager's office until the following day when someone picked it up for the accountant, which is my mom. She paid all the bills and made sure the receipts were correct before we sent it to the bank.

"They?" I turned to Drina who had her head down.

"Lisa was with her."

"Is that why Zakiya was upset?" Drina nodded and I told the guard it's ok.

All the workers were scared to death of us. Plus, we paid them well and they didn't wanna lose any money over Ciara or Lisa's bullshit.

"Spill it." I said putting the key in the ignition.

"Nope."

"Drina don't play with me." She folded her arms across her chest.

"No because you're going to tell him and..."

"Oh, like you told your friend about the cost of the ring." I shook my head.

"That's your fault."

"My fault?" I questioned pulling out the parking lot.

"Yup. Had you not put him on speaker, I wouldn't have heard."

"Are you serious?"

"Yup."

"You petty as hell Drina and you know damn well, you had no business repeating it." She waved me off.

"Tell me what went down in the bathroom." I repeated myself.

She started telling me and all I could do is shake my head. Lisa is pushing my brother and regardless if he cares for her or not, he will take her life.

I parked in front of my crib and walked inside with her damn near stripping before I closed the door.

"Damn Drina." She and I wasted no time doing what we do best.

* * *

"I'm so excited about the baby. Are you?" We just left the doctor's office and found out she's expecting again. A nigga was happy as hell and I know my mother will be. She's been waiting for me to get her pregnant again.

"Hell yea, I'm happy." I responded as I stared at the black SUV following us.

I know it's not the one that crashed into Conscience because the dude is dead, and the truck was totaled. Each turn I took; the SUV did the same. Drina wasn't paying attention because she was on the phone texting.

"GET DOWN!" I shouted when my eyes went to the rear-view mirror and I saw the person pointed a rifle at us. Drina slipped down without asking any questions.

TAT, TAT, TAT, TAT! Is all we heard going up and down streets. I wasn't worried about being hit because the truck is bulletproof. I'm more worried about Drina seeing me blow the guys brains out on the side of us.

He pulled up and pointed straight at me. I have no idea who the individual is, nor did I recognize the driver. With all that's going on, I did wanna know why they were shooting at me. I turned the wheel, hit the truck and watched as it flipped over and landed on its back.

"Don't get out." I told Drina and opened my door. I had my truck up the street a little in case she needed to pull off without me.

"Courage. Let's go. The cops can handle it. Please." She cried.

"Leave if you hear any shooting."

"Babe please get in."

"Lock the doors and let me make sure they're dead. I'll be

right back." I closed the door and aimed my gun towards the car.

Each step I took, I surveyed the area to make sure no one else was coming. I walked up on the truck and made sure my gun went to the window before I did.

"Help me." The driver whispered and reached his hand out. I pulled the door open and drug him out. I placed the gun on his forehead.

"Why you shooting at me?" He coughed up blood.

"Who the fuck are you and who sent you?"

"I'm supposed to kill..." He coughed again.

"Your girlfriend."

"My girlfriend?" I questioned and looked back at the truck Drina was in. I saw her head sticking out the window and tears streaming down her face.

"Did someone pay you to do this?" He nodded. His breaths were very shallow.

"Who?"

"It was..." The nigga stopped speaking and his soul left his body. I rushed back to the truck but didn't make it in time.

"ANDRINAAAAA!" I shouted as another SUV crashed into my truck, pushing it into a tree. This can't be happening.

CHAPTER 24

Conscience

"Has Consequence contacted you yet?" Rock asked standing behind me as I prepared dinner.

"No. It's ok though." He backed away and leaned against the counter.

"I had to put myself in his shoes and if the roles were reversed, I'm sure I'd feel the exact same."

"Would you forgive him?"

"Eventually. After you were better, I'd probably make arrangements to speak on it." I moved around the kitchen.

"My mom said don't rush anything and let it happen when it does." I shrugged.

"What about my cousin?" He folded his arms.

"Consequence said, she's gonna come for me and I respect it. I almost killed her, and retaliation is a must when dealing with someone from the hood." I stopped and turned.

"Before you get upset, I wasn't saying it to be disrespectful.

I just know how we come from different worlds and our thought process isn't the same when someone tries to take your life."

"Is that so?"

"Zakiya doesn't have money, well, she will once my brother marries her. Anyway, she's been in survival mode from what you say all of her life."

"True." He said.?

"Even at the dinner when Consequence first introduced us, one could tell her defense was up." I grabbed some plates to set the table.

He and I had dinner as a family at least three times a week. We were always busy and made a pact to eat dinner together when possible. We both enjoyed it because it gave us time to talk and really appreciate one another.

"I can say, I hate not knowing what she has planned because I can't prepare myself. However; she wasn't prepared the night in question either."

"Do you regret it?" I stopped.

"Of course I do Rock. I mean, right before it happened, we had a decent conversation at the restaurant. Not to mention us speaking at my parents' house. Look." I moved closer to him and wrapped my arms around his body.

"I made a mistake and you were correct. Had I trusted you, none of it would've happened. I'm sorry you're caught in the middle." He leaned down to kiss me.

"Conscience, what you doing for the rest of your life?" He moved me away and got down on one knee.

"From the looks of it; you." He smirked.

"Will you marry me?" He opened the box to showcase a huge ring. It's nothing like the one my mom said Consequence gave Zakiya, but then again no one will ever have a ring like hers because it's one of a kind.

"I thought you didn't wanna marry me. Oh my God yes. Yes baby." I was jumping up and down as he tried to put it on.

"I know I'm not as wealthy as you, but I promise to give you all I have. Conscience..." I shushed him with my lips.

"I don't care if you picked this ring up outta the Kmart jewelry department. I would've still said yes." He lifted me up and wrapped my legs around his waist.

"Whatever I have is yours." He sat me on the island and stared down at me.

"I don't want your money."

"I know baby. I just want you to know that if you did, I'd give it to you." He nodded and slowly undid the buttons on my shirt.

DING! DONG!

"Fuck the door." He said and continued kissing on my neck as he undressed me.

DING! DONG! I let my head fall back in frustration. I wanted this as much as him.

"Go head babe. I'm gonna call my mom and finish setting the table. After dinner, your fiancé is going to do some real nasty things to you." He licked his lips and walked backwards to the door. I picked up the phone and called my mom. When she didn't answer, I left a message for her to call me back.

"Why the fuck you here?" I overheard Rock say. He wasn't yelling but he wasn't quiet either.

"Rock don't be like that." I heard a woman's voice and froze.

I know I promised to trust him but there's no way in hell some chick is at my house for him. I headed towards the door and stopped when I saw the side of her.

The woman was short and dressed decent. Her hair seemed to be freshly done and I couldn't help how she stared angrily at my fiancé.

"Did you tell her about me?"

"No. Why the fuck would I? Look, you have to go." He tried to push her away.

"Is everything ok babe?" The woman turned around and gave me the most hateful glare ever.

"Babe? Is this the bitch?" She pointed to me.

"Yo! Don't call her a bitch. You gotta go."

"Bitch?" I snapped.

"Conscience, I got this."

"Yea, he got this." I stood there watching his interaction with this woman and realized they were well acquainted with one another.

"Rock, who is this?"

"None of your got damn business bitch." The woman fired off. He grabbed her by the shirt.

"Get off me Rock. Fuck this bitch and why haven't you told her about me?" She snatched away and stood directly in front of me. Anger radiated off her body and even though it was barely two seconds, it felt longer as she looked me up and down in disgust.

"Marie, let's go."

"Marie?" I questioned.

"Not until I do this." Before I could speak or even step outta the way, I felt something hard against my head. The woman was swinging it over and over.

"WHAT THE FUCK!" I was dazed and confused.

"Rock, what's going on?" Blood dripped down my eye that was probably split open, and it felt like more blood came from the top of my head as well.

"Fuck! You ok?" He helped me to the couch.

"I'm tired of this shit with her. Tell her who the fuck I am Rock." The woman barked.

"Where the fuck you get a gun from?" He asked, just as she brought it down to my face again and this time, the tip was on my forehead.

"I'm about to blow your fucking brains out and Rock's too, if he tries to stop me." Is the last thing I heard before I succumbed to my facial injuries.

CHAPTER 25
Consequence

"It's been a few days and I'm ready to talk." Zakiya said walking in the bedroom. I smiled staring at her getting comfortable on the bed.

It's been three days since we left the club and she refused to say what went down. Courage called me the following day and told me a little. I asked him not to say too much because to be honest, I wanted her to tell me. I needed her to know she could trust that I'd have her back at all times. Communication is the key and I wanted us to always have it with one another.

"What's up?" I turned the television down and gave her my full attention.

"Why did you ask me to marry you?"

"Is that a trick question?" I asked continuing to smoke my black and mild.

"No. I wanna know the real reason you asked." I blew smoke in the opposite direction.

"I thought I made it clear when I proposed in Italy, but since you need a reminder; let me reiterate it again." I took another pull and put the mild in the ashtray.

"Zakiya, you are a hardheaded, shit talking, think you know it all woman." She folded her arms across her chest.

"You're also a woman with a great heart who cared for my son at a time I couldn't. You know, when you distracted me in the store." She sucked her teeth. I still mess with her about it.

"Anyway, I brought you home to meet my family and you stood your ground through dinner and any other bullshit that came your way." I had her move closer to me.

"Once we had sex, the connection grew stronger and even though we fought to stay away from one another, the chemistry we had, brought us back together. Well that and the shooting." Her facial expression changed to upset.

"You adopted lil Con, moved in with us, and you let me know I can't cheat or disrespect you, which means a lot to a nigga who gave zero fucks." She smirked.

"It's been you and I ever since." I made her have direct eye contact with me.

"I proposed to you Zakiya because I'm truly in love with you and wanna spend the rest of my life with you." I wiped the lone tear falling down her face.

"Are you sure it's not because your sister almost killed me?"

"What? Who the fuck said some shit like that?" My anger went from 0-100 real quick.

"Lisa said..." I cut her off.

"Fuck that bitch."

"You say that, but she continues to bring up the hospital incident and it looks crazy Consequence. How could you sleep with her that night?" I blew my breath and told her the truth.

"When you were shot, she called and asked me to meet outside. She wanted to make sure I was ok and since the doctors had you in surgery, I thought nothing of it. I went out there and she enticed the shit outta me." She rolled her eyes.

"I'm not even gonna front Za. I was stressed out like a motherfucker and messed up. I know it's not an excuse, but I swear after that, I never touched her again. I denied access to her any and everywhere and stripped her of anything I ever gave her." I took her hands in mine.

"She's jealous as fuck of you Zakiya because you're the only woman who actually got me to leave her alone. Hell, Lauren couldn't even get me to stop." I lifted her head that dropped when I mentioned messing up.

"I love you Zakiya and her time is coming to an end soon." I pecked her lips.

"Who told her I was shot?"

"She told me when I walked outside that night. Maybe she saw it in the computer or something. I didn't ask." She nodded.

"Come on." I put the mild out, stood and pulled her up with me.

"Where we going?"

"Out." I threw some sweats and a shirt on and she got dressed too.

"Alma, we'll be back." I yelled out on the way down the stairs. She was cleaning up and lil Con was watching television.

"Where you going?" He questioned and hopped off the couch.

"Out with your mom."

"Can I come?"

"Sure, why not?" He ran to get his sneakers and rushed to Zakiya's side. I swear she spoiled the fuck outta him.

"Let's ride." We all jumped in the truck and left.

* * *

"What are we doing here?" Zakiya asked when we parked in the back of the courthouse.

"I made a call and the mayor is meeting us here." This isn't where his office is, but I wanted this done today and since he was out when I called, it didn't make sense for him to drive back to his office.

"The mayor?" My son asked.

"Yea. We have to get some paperwork processed and..." I lifted Zakiya's hand and kissed it.

"And what?"

"Get married." She gasped and my son jumped up and down.

"But I'm not dressed." She complained like any woman who would having a shotgun wedding.

"You said we can get married anytime and anywhere right?" I reminded her.

"Well yea but..."

"But nothing." The door opened and the mayor stepped aside for us to walk in.

"We have to hurry up because my secretary is in a rush to go home." He chuckled and closed the door behind us. His son is a judge and allowed him to use his office when needed. He brought her as the second witness.

We followed him to the office and filled out the papers he already had waiting. Him and the secretary signed as the witnesses and I let lil Con do it too. He wanted to feel like he was a part of the ceremony.

We didn't recite our own vows because Zakiya wanted to say them at the bigger wedding she said we were having. I didn't care, as long as she's happy, it's the only thing that mattered to me.

"That was fast." Lil Con said making us all laugh.

"Don't worry son. The bigger one will take longer." He smiled and walked over to the secretary and Zakiya, who were talking about something.

"I can't file it until tomorrow, but it'll be legal."

"Thanks for doing this on short notice." I shook his hand.

"Anything for you Mr. Waters. Just make sure your father meets me at the golf course Saturday so I can beat his ass." I started laughing.

As we all walked out together, I couldn't help but feel as if someone were watching me. Zakiya stopped short and grabbed lil Con's hand when we were approached by two big ass dudes. I wasn't worried.

"What can I do for you?" The mayor asked as we moved around them.

I had my son and new wife get in the truck. I gave Zakiya a look and saw her go straight to her phone. I didn't keep secrets from her and explained how someone was after me and if we're ever out and I gave her the look, it meant to contact my brother and Ron. They'd go from there.

"I'll make sure to let my father know what you said." I told the Mayor and before I spoke another word, waited for him and his secretary to leave. I'm not sure what's about to happen, but they didn't need to be caught up in no bullshit.

"You got five seconds to say what you here for or I promise, to blow your fucking head off." I pulled my gun out so fast, neither of them knew what hit em. I didn't wait five seconds because it would've given them time to get me and I was tryna to leave. I wanted to consummate my marriage.

I also didn't want my son to see any of this and hopefully, Zakiya gave him his headphones soon as he got inside the truck as a distraction.

I watched their bodies drop, and a car door opened. I saw the feet and soon the person and shook my head. A bigger dude stepped out on the other side, and his facial expression let me know he's not happy to see me.

"If you're visiting the mayor with that woman it could only mean, you asked her to marry you or you're here to get papers to do it."

"What the fuck you want?" I barked and pointed my gun at

him. I'm not sure he's holding but I ain't taking no chances either.

"I was just wondering how you can marry another woman, when we're still married?" Lauren had the nerve to smirk.

"Consequence, you're still married?" I heard Zakiya ask and turned my head for one second. Why did I do that? All hell broke loose.

To Be Continued....

Now Available on Amazon

Available on Amazon

Made in United States
North Haven, CT
11 May 2024